It was completely quiet, but as soon as I opened the door the Jack Russell terrier in the first kennel started barking. He set off the collie in the kennel next door, and she set off the Staffy opposite.

Once they started, the rest all followed – all except Gus. When I reached his kennel he was standing exactly where I'd left him, still shivering.

'Come on, boy,' I said, 'you're not staying here for one more minute.' And with that I put him back on the lead and walked him straight out of that draughty old kennel block.

Melissa Wareham always dreamed of owning her own dog. But it was only ever a dream until the day General Gus arrives at the rescue home she works for. Gus, a gorgeous, elderly mongrel, who needs a new home. Needs someone to love, and to love him . . .

Rescuing Gus

Gus

Melissa Wareham

RED FOX BOOKS

RED FOX

UK | USA | Canada | Ireland | Australia
India | New Zealand | South Africa

Puffin Books is part of the Penguin Random House group of companies
whose addresses can be found at global.penguinrandomhouse.com.

www.penguin.co.uk
www.puffin.co.uk
www.ladybird.co.uk

Penguin
Random House
UK

This edition published 2013

001

Set in 14/20pt Bembo by Falcon Oast Graphic Art Ltd
Printed in Great Britain by Clays Ltd, St Ives plc

A CIP catalogue record for this book is available from the British Library

ISBN: 978–1–782–95669–3

All correspondence to:
Red Fox
Penguin Random House Children's
80 Strand, London WC2R 0RL

MIX
Paper from
responsible sources
FSC® C018179

For Max, Lilly, Tom,
Phoebe and Harry

CHAPTER ONE

A Canine Criminal

'Am I adopted?' I asked my mum when I was nine years old.

'Why on earth do you ask that?' she said.

'Because dogs are my favourite things in the whole world and you and Dad hate them.'

'We don't hate them,' she said. 'We just—' She stopped in mid-sentence.

'Just what?' I asked, eager to understand.

'Just . . . don't want all the hair, slobber and mess.'

But she hadn't answered my question and it suddenly all made perfect sense. From that moment on I was sure I must be adopted. How could someone who adored dogs as much as me possibly belong to these people who just thought dogs were hairy, smelly, pooing machines?

'But don't you want to be greeted by a friendly face and a waggy tail every time you come through the front door?' I asked, still trying to make them see sense.

'No, thank you,' said my dad matter-of-factly.

'I bet my *real* parents have got a dog; I bet they've got four or five!' I said in a huff.

'*Right!*' said my mum and stormed off. She returned five minutes later holding a crumpled piece of paper. 'Here,' she said, thrusting my birth certificate under my nose. 'Tough luck; you're ours and we're yours!'

OK, so I wasn't adopted; I just had strange parents. I mean, who on earth doesn't want a dog?

Strange people, that's who!

★

From the age of three I had begged my mum and dad for a dog. My entire childhood was spent pleading and bargaining with them. I did the washing-up, took the rubbish out, tidied my room and cleaned out every single goldfish tank we ever owned. All for nothing; but I wouldn't give up. If I couldn't have my own dog, I'd have the next best thing, and as soon as I left school I went to work at Battersea Dogs Home, an animal shelter in the heart of London that cares for 600 lost and abandoned dogs. It was the only place I could think of where I'd be surrounded by hundreds of dogs, all day, every day.

I loved working there so much it wasn't even like a proper job – I would have done it for free if anybody had asked me to! Every minute of every day I was within cuddling distance of something four-legged and furry. Big dogs with warm velvet ears, medium dogs with soft shaggy fur and small dogs I could carry around inside my coat, their little hearts beating against mine.

Having all those dogs around me was brilliant but I knew I'd never be able to have my own dog until I moved out of my parents' home; only then would I finally be able to fulfil my lifelong dream. So, a year after starting work at the dogs' home, I packed up my few belongings, said goodbye to my parents (still wondering if they'd forged my birth certificate) and off I went.

It was an otherwise ordinary Monday morning. I was late as usual – my alarm clock just wasn't as effective as my mum yelling at me and dragging the duvet off my bed. I raced into work and was greeted by the usual cacophony of barking dogs.

My kennel block was the biggest in the whole dogs' home. It was as long and as wide as a swimming pool but thankfully a lot drier! It had a narrow corridor down the middle with forty kennels on either side, each one a temporary home for one, two or sometimes even three dogs. Every kennel had metal bars at the front and sides, running all the way from the floor to the ceiling. The back of the kennel was a brick wall.

'Morning, boys and girls!' I shouted, trying to make myself heard. It was a cold February morning and the day's new arrivals had just started coming in. They were mainly strays, found wandering the streets of London, shivering. Some were lost, some abandoned.

Once they were safely inside the dogs' home they could be collected by their owners. If their owners didn't want them or couldn't look after them any more, it was up to me and the other people who worked at Battersea Dogs Home to find them new owners. I had no idea when I walked into work on that ordinary Monday morning that, before long, one of those new owners would be me!

When all the morning's new arrivals were safely tucked into their kennels, I decided it was time to meet them. They were a noisy bunch, and as I walked down the corridor I saw dogs of all different colours, shapes and sizes:

- huge pony-sized dogs
- tiny rabbit-sized dogs
- fat pig-sized dogs
- spaghetti-thin dogs
- old grey dogs
- young bouncy dogs
- chocolate-brown dogs
- snowy-white dogs
- liquorice-black dogs
- spotty dotty dogs
- shaggy mop-haired dogs

As I was walking through the kennels, I noticed my shoelace was undone. I knelt down to tie the loose lace and heard a sort of squeaky snorting very close to my left ear. I turned my head and there he was, staring straight back at me through the bars of his kennel.

He was mostly black, had big chocolate-coloured eyes, pointy ears that flopped over at the ends and a grey face with long white whiskers. And even though he was sitting on his long black bushy tail, it was wagging like mad!

'Hello,' I said through the bars, 'I haven't seen you before. You must be a new boy; what's your name then?'

I didn't really expect him to answer – if he had I probably would have had a heart attack! I unclipped the card from his kennel door and began to read.

NAME: Unknown
NUMBER: 2364
BREED: Part mongrel, part husky
COLOUR: Black with white chest and grey face
SEX: Male
AGE: Unknown (but looks elderly!)
HISTORY: Prisoner's Property

*

'Hmm, Prisoner's Property, eh?' I said to him. 'Have you been up to no good then, boy?'

'That is correct,' I heard a voice say. I nearly had that heart attack! My mouth fell open and I stared at the dog.

'Ahem,' came a cough from behind me. I spun round and was relieved to see a policeman standing there. 'You OK?' he asked me.

'Yes, sorry, I thought the dog . . . never mind, how can I help you, Officer?' I asked.

'Well, I've just brought this furry four-legged fellow into the kennels,' he said, nodding towards the black dog with the grey face, 'and I thought you might want to know a bit about him.'

'Oh, yes please,' I answered. 'It says on his card that he's a prisoner's property.'

'He certainly is,' replied the policeman. 'His owner is Jimmy Stickles, a local car thief. I caught Jimmy red-handed in the driver's seat of a stolen car. He was looking very shifty, and sitting next to him, safely strapped behind the seat belt of the passenger seat was this here hound. The dog was looking just as shifty,' the policeman added, looking rather pleased with himself, 'so I had no choice but to arrest them both.'

'You arrested a dog?' I said, more than a little surprised. I looked through the bars at the canine criminal whose long pink tongue was dangling down from his white-whiskered chops. 'You wouldn't make a very good getaway driver,' I said to him. 'For starters, your paws wouldn't reach the pedals!' But he wasn't laughing and neither was the policeman.

The officer continued, 'Like I said, I had no choice but to arrest the man *and* his dog, and now they're both behind bars. We think Jimmy will be in prison for a very long time.'

'But what's going to happen to his dog?' I asked, kneeling down and looking at the dog through the kennel bars. It was clear that this particular pooch was neither lost nor abandoned, but his owner wouldn't be able to look after him any more, so here he was – locked in a kennel, frightened and alone.

The policeman shrugged. 'His family can have him if they want him. They've got twenty-eight days to decide.'

All of the dogs that came in that day were beautiful in their own way, but there was something extra special about that floppy-eared four-legged car thief! He was ever so handsome and seemed to be smiling at me, like he wanted to be friends.

I read his card again:

BREED: Part mongrel, part husky

'Mongrel, hey?' I said to him. 'Yes, I can see you're a mixture of lots of different breeds.' But of all those breeds I could definitely see husky the most and could imagine him pulling a sled in the snow with a load of his husky mates.

Thankfully there was no snow in the kennel, but I was glad he had his big black fur coat on – it was a little on the draughty side in there.

NUMBER: 2364

That meant he was the two thousand, three hundred and sixty-fourth dog that had arrived at the dogs' home since the 1st of January. That was a lot of unwanted dogs; after all, it was only February now!

'Well,' I said to him, 'I can't call you *Number 2364*, can I? Let's give you a proper name, shall we?' I took a step back and looked at him. '*George?*' I said, and he tilted his head to the left. 'No, you're not a George, are you? What about *Gordon?*' He sneezed his displeasure. 'No, I don't think so either.'

Hmm. This was a very important decision and we had to get it right.

'*Got it!* How about *Gus?*' And he stood up and wagged his tail approvingly. 'Yes, I like it too,' I said. 'It makes you sound wise and handsome.'

Gus and I were getting to know each other when we were rudely interrupted by Henry, the big fat Labrador in the next-door kennel. He'd started barking his head off – probably hungry again – and once Henry started barking, all the other dogs did too. Gus must have thought he was in a madhouse – here he was in the middle of a kennel block with a hundred howling hounds. And never mind the noise, what about the smell? Gus's hooter was bombarded with all sorts of strange pongs: disinfectant, dog food, wee, poo, air-freshener and dogs dogs dogs. Scared dogs, happy dogs, sleepy dogs, mean dogs, poorly dogs and friendly dogs – all mixed up together, all trying to make sense of their crazy new surroundings.

'*AAAWWOOOOOOOOOO!*' Gus had decided to join in.

'Do you need an emergency cuddle?' I asked, and he pawed the front of his kennel. 'OK, boy,

I'm coming in.' Once inside, I knelt down to stroke him. He was warm and soft, but he was shaking slightly. He climbed into my lap, which wasn't easy as he was too big to be a lap dog! At that moment, I couldn't help falling a little bit in love with old Gus.

My fellow kennel maid, Karen, walked into the block balancing a tower of food bowls in her arms. 'Who's your friend?' she asked whilst dishing out breakfast. Henry hoovered his up in less than five seconds.

'I don't know his real name, but I've decided he looks like a *Gus*,' I replied. 'What do you think, Karen?'

She looked at him for a while and then declared, 'He looks a bit like my friend's granddad. He's a general in the army and he's got grey whiskers too! *General Gus* – perfect!'

'Gus is a *Prisoner's Property* dog,' I said, 'so he could be with us for four whole weeks while his owner's family decide if they want him or not.'

Four weeks – that did sound like a long time. Gus's tail suddenly drooped and he looked up at me with big, round, sad eyes. Could he understand me?

I put a blanket in his bed and gave him a bowl of food, but he wasn't interested in it. He didn't even sniff the food; he just curled up on his blanket and let out a long sigh. Hmm, I'd have to keep a very close eye on poor old General Gus.

A week went by and Gus was not a happy chappie. He'd hardly eaten anything and didn't look like he'd slept much either. Then something rather unexpected happened. Gus had a visitor – a human visitor.

It was Jimmy Stickles's mum. I held my breath. Perhaps she had come to take him home. I would miss Gus terribly, but it would be better for him to be out of the kennels and back with his family. I crossed my fingers behind my back.

'Look who's come to see you, boy,' I said to Gus, and he lifted his chin up off the floor. When he saw Jimmy's mum standing right there in front of him holding a blue teddy bear, he couldn't believe his eyes. He shot out of his bed and ran towards her. His tail was wagging so hard I wondered if he might take off like a helicopter! I'd never seen him look so happy. He was squealing with delight.

'Hello, darling,' Jimmy's mum said to him. 'I've brought you your favourite teddy.' She handed Gus his bear, which he gently took in his mouth. She knelt down and gave him a big hug, but when he crawled into her lap she began sneezing.

AAACCCHHHOOOOOOO!

'Now listen, boy,' she said, blowing her nose, 'you know I'd take you home to live with me if I could, but I'm allergic to you so it'd never work. I just wanted to bring you your teddy.'

AAACCCHHHOOOOOOO!

She sneezed another mighty sneeze and blew

her nose again, this time so hard the tissue flew out of her hand and landed on Gus's left ear. He shook it off and stared up at her.

'I'm sorry, boy, I've got to go now but I know you'll find a nice new home,' she said, blowing into a fresh, clean tissue. 'Goodbye, sweetheart. I'll miss you.' And with that she kissed the top of his head and walked away.

Gus's tail instantly stopped wagging. It looked like it might never wag again!

I caught up with her. 'Hang on a minute,' I said. 'Isn't there anyone else in your family who might want him? He hates it here in the kennels.'

'Well,' she said, thinking hard, 'there's Jimmy's girlfriend, Stacey, but she doesn't really like dogs. She says they have dog breath.' *Of course they have dog breath*, I thought to myself, *they're dogs!*

'There's Jimmy's older brother, Dave,' she continued, 'but he's already got two terriers and they're not too keen on other dogs. Jimmy's sister Sue wouldn't have him; she still hasn't forgiven him for running off with the turkey last Christmas!'

I looked down at Gus. *Honestly, nicking cars* and *turkeys!* He looked away as though ashamed of his criminal behaviour.

Jimmy's mum blew her nose again. 'Jimmy's gran would have him in a heartbeat, but she's not allowed dogs in her little flat.' She held my arm and said, 'It's a terrible thing – we'll all miss him, you know. Please take good care of him while he's with you in the kennels and try to find him a nice home. He's such a good boy.'

She signed the papers handing Gus over to the dogs' home and walked off in a hurry. 'Wait,' I called after her. 'What's his real name?'

But she was gone. I never saw her again, and neither did Gus.

Gus had loved seeing Jimmy's mum so much and having his teddy was a comfort, but in some ways seeing her had only made him sadder. His feelings were all tangled up, like they'd been through the washing machine.

If Gus's family didn't want him, then we'd just have to find him a new home. It wouldn't be easy though – not many people wanted older dogs; they all wanted puppies.

I looked at Gus and he looked at me. It was as though the same thought had just gone through his mind too. Suddenly Gus's future looked very bleak.

Things had to improve, and fast. Thankfully his luck was about to change, and soon he'd have more than just his blue teddy bear to put a smile on his furry face.

CHAPTER TWO

Coughs, Snots and Bogies

Gus wouldn't eat the dog food we gave him – but he was so sad that I didn't blame him – so I tried to tempt him with different types of yummy human food. So far, I'd offered him:

- peanut butter on toast
- chicken nuggets
- custard
- fish fingers
- chips

- spaghetti hoops
- cheese
- hamburgers
- steak . . .

He turned his nose up at all of them, except the cheese. What food should I have tried him on? What food would *you* have given Gus?

Since his arrival, Gus had hardly eaten anything, so it was lucky he was a little podgy when he first came into the kennels otherwise he'd have looked like a whippet by now!

I was determined to cheer up my favourite car-stealing hound though, so I tried other ways to make him feel happy. I cuddled him, played with him, took him for walks, brushed him and even bought him a squeaky toy hamburger, but he wasn't in the mood to play.

No, I'd have to try another tactic.

'I've got an idea,' I said to Karen. 'I think Gus needs a friend.'

I went to fetch Arty, a young, goofy bulldog.

Arty was very funny – he snorted through his squashed-up nose, wagged his stumpy little tail and bounced all over the place like a kangaroo who'd sat on a bee! But he didn't make Gus laugh *or* cheer him up. Quite the opposite. He bounced on top of Gus and licked his face all over with his stinky dog tongue. Gus must have felt like he was in a car wash!

'*Arty!*' I yelled. 'Be gentle – Gus isn't a bouncy castle, you know!' But Arty wasn't listening; he was off again, bouncing his way around Gus's kennel. This wasn't working. I waded in, grabbed Arty and put him back in his own kennel next door. 'Well, that experiment didn't work, did it!' I said to Karen.

Finding Gus some doggy company was proving just as hard as finding him some food he wanted to eat, but I wasn't going to give up. After the bulldog-shaped disaster it would have to be someone smaller and calmer next time . . .

Aha! Mini the Chihuahua would be perfect.

Mini was the tiniest dog in the whole dogs' home, and one thing was for sure – she wouldn't bounce all over Gus like Arty did.

I brought her into Gus's kennel. At first he wasn't even sure she was a dog. You couldn't blame him; you see, she was so small that none of the dog coats in the cupboard fitted her, so I had made her a special coat out of one of my big pink woolly bed socks. It fitted Mini perfectly, but made her look more like a worm with legs than a dog!

Just like lots of small dogs, Mini had a big attitude and the first thing she did was bark loudly at Gus. He nearly jumped out of his fur and shot into the corner of the kennel, refusing to come out. How could a wise and terribly important dog like General Gus be scared of this teeny tiny terror? Perhaps he thought she was a mouse. Whatever it was, he stuck in his corner and wouldn't budge. This wasn't exactly love at first sight so I took Mini out again. We were back to square one.

The next morning I was in bright and early.

'Morning, Gus!' I said cheerily. 'I've brought you something extra tasty for your breakfast; last night's home-made shepherd's pie with extra gravy.' I put the bowl down in front of him. 'It's my mum's special recipe and I'm so sure you'll eat it I've told Karen that if you don't I'll eat a spoonful of your dog food!' Karen was watching intently from outside the kennel, a tin of dog food at the ready.

Gus was in bed with his teddy and didn't even get up to sniff the shepherd's pie.

I knelt down and stroked him. 'Come on, boy, you've got to eat something,' I said, and then whispered, 'and you wouldn't want me to have to eat dog food, would you?'

Suddenly Gus lifted his head up and began sniffing the air. I was saved!

'That's it boy, it's right here,' I said, moving the bowl closer to him.

But Gus wasn't sniffing the shepherd's pie.

He walked round to my other side, sniffed some more, put his head in my coat pocket and gently pulled out my lunch banana. He held it in his mouth and wagged his tail furiously. Well, at least it was my banana he was pinching and not my purse! He still hadn't touched the shepherd's pie but I didn't even care – I was just *so* pleased to see Gus wagging his tail.

Karen began opening the tin of dog food. 'I hope you're hungry,' she said to me with an evil grin on her face.

I tried to ignore her and turned to Gus. 'You want my banana?' I asked him. He wagged harder so that his whole bum swayed from side to side. I peeled it and held it out to him. He wolfed it down in one go. *Bingo!*

'That's it!' I said to Karen. 'I've found it; I've found Gus's favourite food. It's bananas!'

'Bananas?' Karen replied. 'Who ever heard of a dog eating bananas? Mind you, who's ever heard of a human eating dog food?' she added, grinning, and handed me a spoonful. I held my breath and took a small nibble. Actually, it wasn't bad. It tasted a bit like steak and kidney pie but without the pastry.

We were making some progress but it was slow going. We hadn't managed to find Gus a new home yet – people would walk up to his kennel, but when they saw an old dog they just kept on walking. At least Gus had his blue teddy, which he loved, and his bananas, which were the highlight of his day – but he *hated* being locked in a kennel. I still hadn't given up on the idea of finding Gus a kennel mate, and decided it was time to go and get another next-door neighbour – Henry.

Henry the chocolate-coloured Labrador was huge, round and brown, and looked rather a lot like an Easter egg with a tail. He was much calmer than Arty and much more Gus's size than Mini. But best of all, Henry loved other dogs and other dogs loved Henry. Maybe they thought he really was a chocolate Easter egg!

I unlocked Gus's kennel. 'Gus, meet Henry. Henry, meet Gus.'

Gus's tail started wagging. *Brilliant*, I thought to myself, *this is really going to work!* But instead of going over to Gus for a sniff, which is the usual doggy way of saying hello, Henry spotted all the bowls of uneaten food that I'd been trying to tempt Gus with.

Oh no! Labradors *love* food, and true enough Henry completely forgot about Gus and dived straight into every single bowl. He hoovered up their contents with such gusto that Gus looked a little worried Henry might hoover him up too!

Once all the food was gone, Henry searched the whole kennel from top to bottom looking for any little scraps he might have missed. He up-ended Gus's water bowl *and* his bed. When he saw Gus's squeaky toy hamburger Henry thought his luck was in and he pounced on it, gobbling it up whole!

'*Henry, no!*' Karen and I yelled at the same

time. Henry suddenly looked a little sick, and when he tried to bark the only sound that came out was the squeak from the toy!

I pulled Henry out and put him back in the kennel next door. Gus must have thought he was surrounded by lunatics. There was Henry, the world's fattest, hungriest, and now squeakiest Labrador on one side, and Arty the incredible bouncing bulldog on the other side.

But Arty was under the weather and had lost most of his bounce. He'd been sneezing all morning and wasn't fussy about which direction he aimed his sneezes. Just then, Arty turned towards Gus, took a deep breath, and through the kennel bars sneezed the biggest, loudest sneeze ever, right over Gus!

Poor Gus. Not only was he sad and lonely, but now he was soaking wet *and* covered in a layer of green slimy snot.

Three days later and it wasn't just Arty that was as sick as a dog. Two long elastic stalactites of snot hung down from Gus's nostrils, and when he moved his head they swung from left to right like a clock pendulum. He had a terrible cough too, and when he hacked he sounded more like a sea lion than a dog. Sure enough, Arty had given Gus his cold. Arty was already taking tablets to make him better, and now it was time to take Gus to see the dog doctor.

'Come in,' said the vet after I'd knocked on his door for five whole minutes. He was a little deaf.

'*Well, hello there!*' he yelled, louder than he needed to. '*And who do we have here, then?*'

'Hello, sir,' I said. 'This is Gus.'

'*Russ?*'

'No, Gus.'

'*Ah, Buzz,*' he said, lowering his voice so as not to frighten the dog. 'And what seems to be the trouble with Buzz?'

'*Gus* has a bad cold,' I said, shouting his name in the hope the vet would get it. 'I think it might even be the flu.'

'Well, pop Buzz on the table then and we'll take a look,' said the friendly old vet. He had a full head of white hair and a beard to match. While he examined Gus it suddenly dawned on me that dog and vet looked identical. They both had furry white faces and bushy eyebrows! I couldn't control myself and burst out laughing.

The vet looked at me over the top of his glasses as though I'd gone mad.

'Sorry,' I said, stifling a snigger.

The vet took Gus's temperature and at that moment I was very glad I wasn't a dog. When I was sick, my mum used to put a thermometer under my tongue to take my temperature. Most dogs would probably try to eat a thermometer if it was put in their mouth so instead the thermometer has to go up the dog's bum! Thank goodness only vets can do this so I didn't have to!

'Yes,' said the vet. 'Buzz's temperature is quite high. Is he off his food?' he asked.

'He's off his bananas,' I said to the vet, who

I'm sure probably thought the same about me!

'Even though he has a snotty nose and a hacking cough, he hasn't quite got the flu,' said the vet, 'but it's very similar. It's sort of the doggy version of flu and it's called *kennel cough*. It's nothing to worry about; we'll give him some tablets and some cough mixture and he'll be as right as rain in a week or so.'

Cough mixture for dogs, I thought. *How funny!*

The vet pulled a stethoscope out of the drawer and stuck it in his ears. Gus was standing on the table, patiently allowing the vet to examine him all over. His furry white face was at the same level as mine and I kissed the top of Gus's head. Over the past two weeks, I'd become rather attached to this handsome, homeless hound.

The vet put the other end of the stethoscope to Gus's chest and listened intently. 'Oh dear,' he said, 'oh dear, oh dear, oh dear.'

'What?' I asked, starting to feel a little worried.

'What?' he replied.

'I said, *what*?' I repeated.

'What? Speak up, girl.'

I grabbed the end of the stethoscope and yelled, '*Oh dear, what?*' down it.

'All right,' he said sharply. 'No need to shout!' He took the stethoscope out of his ears and turned to me. 'This poor fellow has a very bad heart murmur, which means his heart isn't working properly. Listen,' he said, and passed me the stethoscope. I put it in my ears and placed the other end on Gus's chest. I couldn't even hear a heart, let alone a heart murmur.

'I can't hear anything,' I said.

The vet moved the stethoscope up a little higher. 'Try now,' he said. 'Can you hear his heartbeat?'

I could.

'Can you hear that it's not quite a proper *boom boom*, *boom boom*. Rather it's a *boom boom* with a sort of whooshing sound as well?' he asked.

I could.

'What does this mean?' I asked the vet, suddenly terrified Gus was going to conk out at any moment.

'Well,' he said, 'it's quite a bad heart murmur. We usually grade them one to six with six being the very worst.'

'What is Gus's?' I asked, praying it would be grade one, two or three.

'Grade five,' he replied, 'and on top of that, Buzz has a few other problems to deal with.'

I stared at Gus; suddenly he looked as though he had the weight of the world on his shoulders. I pulled a tissue from my pocket and wiped his nose.

The vet opened Gus's mouth and looked inside. Phew! What a whiff! I was nearly floored by the stink; it was a cross between blue cheese and old socks.

'Look at his teeth,' the vet said to me.

I held my breath and peered into Gus's mouth. His two big top teeth were worn right down, and instead of being the size of a jelly baby, they were about half the size. It was the same with his two big bottom teeth. The rest were mostly brown and yellow and yucky, and some were even broken.

'Oh, Gus,' I said, 'you haven't been flossing, have you?' I couldn't hold my breath any more so I gently closed his mouth.

'The terrible state his teeth are in shows that he's quite an old dog,' said the vet.

'How old?' I asked.

'Well, we can't know for sure,' he replied, 'but I'd guess Buzz is probably about ten years old.'

'*Ten!?*' I said. 'I didn't think he was that old.' I did some quick maths in my head. I knew that one human year was the same as seven dog years. So if Gus were human he'd be ten times seven, which would make him . . . *seventy years old*!!!! 'Holy bangers and mash; he's as old as my granddad!' I said.

'And that's not all,' said the vet. 'His kennel

cough will be putting a terrible strain on his heart.'

'And there's something else,' I added helpfully. 'His rotten teeth.'

The vet nodded thoughtfully. 'I have to be honest with you,' he said, suddenly looking very serious. 'Old Buzz isn't a puppy any more, and it's hard to say how long he has left.'

Wow, that was hard to hear, certainly for me, but what about Gus? How much bad news could one dog take?

Right at that moment, as though in agreement, Gus gave an almighty sneeze, covering the examination table in thick, green snot.

'Kennel life isn't doing Buzz any good,' said the vet. *You're telling me!* I'd seen Gus every single day since he came in and I knew he hated it in here. 'He needs to get out and spend whatever time he has left in a warm, loving home,' the vet added.

'But his owner's in prison and his family doesn't want him any more,' I told him.

'Poor old fellow,' said the vet, rubbing Gus's ear. 'You shouldn't be here in a draughty old dogs' home at your time of life, boy; you should be at home, lying in front of a fire with a cup of tea.'

A picture of Gus snoozing in front of a roaring log fire, lapping up a saucer of warm tea and wearing slippers suddenly popped into my head!

'How are we doing with finding him a *new* home?' asked the vet.

'Not so well,' I replied. 'No one wants old dogs.'

'What? No one wants gold dogs?' he said, baffled.

'No, not gold dogs, *old dogs*!'

'Yes,' he agreed. 'I've never understood that. Most people want puppies or young dogs, but they are such hard work. They poo everywhere, chew up all your favourite things, run away in the park and are always full of naughtiness. Give me an oldie any day.'

'Me too,' I replied. 'They don't chew

everything in sight, they only poo where they're meant to, they've already been trained and they know so many cool tricks.'

The vet took off his glasses, put them on the side and left the room to get Gus some tablets. I couldn't resist it – I picked up the glasses and put them on Gus's face. It was amazing; he and the vet looked just like twins! I heard the vet's footsteps coming back and quickly replaced the glasses, all the while giggling to myself.

The vet came back in, handed me two bottles of pills and said, 'Give Buzz three tablets twice a day; that's two for his kennel cough and one for his heart. And for goodness sake, find him a home quickly.'

'I'll try my best,' I said.

'Yes, you're right,' he murmured, 'and plenty of rest.'

I led Gus back to my kennel block. He walked slowly and with his head hung low. We had to stop three times so he could cough (once) and sneeze (twice). I unlocked the kennel door and took him over to his bed.

'You'll be OK, boy,' I said to him, but I wasn't sure I believed it. Gus was very sick.

By now it was 5 p.m., dark outside and freezing cold inside. I unclipped Gus's lead, left the kennel and turned around to say goodnight. Gus stood there, shivering. He looked up at me with big round pleading eyes.

'Night, Gus. See you in the morning.'

I walked to the end of the kennel block, turned out the lights and closed the door behind me. I got into my car, slammed the door and turned on the engine. But then something strange happened. I just couldn't seem to drive away. I turned the engine off, got out of the car and walked back up to the kennel block.

It was completely quiet, but as soon as I opened the door the Jack Russell terrier in the first kennel started barking. He set off the collie in the kennel next door, and she set off the Staffy opposite.

Once they started, the rest all followed – all except Gus. When I reached his kennel he was standing exactly where I'd left him, still shivering.

'Come on, boy,' I said, 'you're not staying here for one more minute.' And with that I put him back on the lead and walked him straight out of that draughty old kennel block. Henry and Arty were somehow sleeping through the din, but all the other dogs were barking their heads off and seemed to be saying:

- Hey, where's he going?
- Has his owner come for him?
- What about me?
- Take me too!
- I'll behave myself, honest!
- Why can't I come?
- What's so special about *him*?

I wasn't sure exactly what *was* so special about him. Perhaps it was Gus's age, perhaps it was because he was so sick, maybe it was his heart murmur or the fact his owner was in prison and his family didn't want him.

Whatever it was, from that moment on I knew that Gus was *my* dog. I didn't care that he wasn't a bouncy puppy and wouldn't live for years and years – I'd make sure he was happy and looked-after and he'd never have to go back inside a draughty old kennel again.

He had me and I had him. And just like that, I'd finally fulfilled my lifelong dream; I had my very own dog.

CHAPTER THREE

Home is Where the Hound is

It was a freezing cold February evening, and even though Gus had his own built-in fur coat, he needed an extra layer to keep out the wicked winter wind. I grabbed a dog jumper from the cupboard at the end of the block, and before venturing outside I tried my best to wrestle him into it.

This was easier said than done. To get Gus into the jumper, I had to put it over his head, but all he saw was a big woolly black hole looming towards him. He decided this wasn't for him and quickly began to reverse. I tried and failed three times. If I couldn't put his coat on the normal way, I'd have to do it from back to front.

I started by lifting Gus's two back legs through the hole his head was supposed to go through. Next I pulled the jumper over his bum and up along his back. Then I put his front two legs through the front arm holes and finally pulled the jumper up round his neck. Done: perfect fit!

The jumper was thick, woolly and grey (a bit like Gus!) and reminded me of an old school jumper. He looked down at his new sweater and then back up at me with disapproving eyes.

'Oh, don't look at me like that,' I said to him. 'It'll do for now!' Besides, this wasn't about fashion – it was about keeping my sick dog warm.

I stuffed Gus's teddy into my pocket and we left the kennels behind. We walked towards the car and as I held the door open for Gus to jump in, I had to pinch myself to make sure I wasn't dreaming. I'd dreamed of having a dog for ever and I couldn't believe my dream was finally coming true.

Working at the dogs' home, I had the pick of 600 dogs. I could have chosen:

- a pair of pedigree puppies
- a labradoodle
- a great big Great Dane
- a shaggy sheepdog
- a cockerpoodle
- a springy springer spaniel . . .

. . . but I looked over my shoulder, and sitting in the back seat of my car was an old black granddad mongrel mixed with a little bit of husky, who had floppy ears, a grey face, bad breath, the flu and a wonky heart! How did that happen?

I wasn't sure I'd done the right thing but I *was* sure that Gus *needed* me. Right at this moment, when he'd been abandoned by his family and was sick and alone, he needed someone to love him, and that someone was me.

I knew I'd never leave Gus in the same way some people abandoned their dogs. I'd seen so many owners dump their animals at the dogs' home because they couldn't look after them any more. If I'd learned one thing, it was that dogs were a big, long-term commitment and you had to be in the right situation to be able to look after them properly.

I looked over at my commitment. He was sneezing all over the windows. It was bad enough that thick, green snot was sliding down the glass, but now Gus was licking it up!

'Oh, that's *disgusting*!' I said to him. 'I offered you alphabetti spaghetti *and* chips earlier today, and you'd rather eat snot?!' He looked at me as if to say, yup.

Some dogs have never been in a car before, so those big metal monsters with their noisy engines, loud horns and flashing lights can be quite frightening. Gus, however, seemed very settled on the back seat of my car; it was as though he'd always been around them. And then I remembered – he had. He'd been in a car when he was arrested!

'We're not going out on a job now, you know, Gus,' I said sternly to him. 'Your criminal days are behind you!'

I turned on the engine and we drove home, with Gus occasionally sneezing into the back of my head. By the time we got home my hair was so wet I felt like I'd done twenty laps at the local swimming pool.

'Right, boy,' I said, unlocking my front door, 'welcome to your new home.'

Gus charged through the door as though he owned the place! He explored every little corner of my flat, which didn't take long as it was only small. First he darted into the bedroom – all good; then through into the bathroom – perfectly acceptable; and then into the kitchen – a little small but it'll do.

So far so good.

He finished off his tour in the living room by flipping over onto his back and rolling around on the floor.

'Hey, what are you doing?' I said, more than a little surprised, at which he began wiping his face all over my carpet! Hmm, discovering Gus's strange doggy ways was going to be very interesting.

The good thing was that this was as perky as I'd ever seen Gus. Even though he obviously still had his cough, he seemed so much happier here in a home than in the kennels. Carpet underfoot seemed to suit him better than concrete. Perhaps I should see if he'd eat something? I had some left-over chicken in the fridge, so I warmed it up, put it in one of my cereal bowls and gave it to him. I sneakily hid two of his tablets inside the chicken, hoping he wouldn't notice them. He didn't, and quicker than I could say *hungry hound* he'd wolfed down the lot.

'Hang on a minute,' I said. 'I gave you

chicken yesterday and you turned your nose up at it.' Gus didn't hear me; he was too busy seeing if he'd left any behind. I was delighted he was eating again and looked into the bowl to make sure he'd had it all. He had – except for his two tablets! *Sneaky* – he was cleverer than I thought.

I had to think hard to try and outwit him. I reached into the fruit bowl, pulled out a banana, cut a piece off and stuffed the tablets deep inside.

'Mmm, what's this?' I said to him. He looked interested. 'Ooh, yummy!' I said, and pretended to eat it. Gus jumped up at me. 'You want some, boy?' He was dancing around on the spot. 'Sit.' He sat. 'Give paw.' He practically gave me a high-five so I tossed the banana up in the air. He caught it mid-flight and swallowed it whole.

Yes! Humans–1, Dogs–0. I was officially cleverer than my dog.

With the tablets swallowed by Gus, all I had

to do now was get the cough mixture down him. The vet had given me a device with which to squirt the syrup down his throat. This was going to be fun.

I opened up his mouth. 'Phwoar, Gus, your breath doesn't half pong!' I said, aiming the squirter into the stinky black hole.

I must have offended him, because just as I squirted he clamped his jaws shut and the thick pink liquid went all over him and bounced back all over me too!

'Thanks, Gus.' I wiped us both off with kitchen roll and had another go – but Gus was ready for me. His jaws were shut tight! 'We can either do this the easy way or the hard way,' I said to him. 'It's up to you.' I didn't really have a plan for either way, but it seemed like the right thing to say at that moment. We stared each other out. I thought hard. *I know . . . !*

I got another small piece of banana, threw it in the air, and just as he opened up his mouth to catch it, I squirted the cough mixture in.

Humans–2, Dogs–0!

As soon as the syrup had gone in, he shut his mouth straight away and the banana bounced off the top of his nose and onto the kitchen floor. He hoovered it up and quickly forgot about the nasty pink syrup. Thank goodness for bananas; not only were they my new best friend's best friend; they were *my* new best friend too!

I didn't know whether it was being in a warm home or feeling carpet under his feet or just being with me, but after just a few hours Gus seemed like a different dog. In the kennels he was miserable, quiet and sad, but here in my small flat he was practically turning cartwheels!

'You haven't been faking it, have you?' I asked him, and in reply he sneezed another giant sneeze. This time the snot landed on my television. 'I'll take that as a no, then.'

Gus decided to settle down for the evening and chose my coat to flop onto. I had a bad habit of coming home, taking my coat off and dropping it on the floor. Luckily I didn't live with my mum any more, otherwise I'd be in trouble for sure. Mind you, if I still lived with my mum, there wouldn't be a dirty great hound sneezing all over the living room!

Poor Gus didn't really have anything else to curl up on; he and I had left the dogs' home in such a hurry I'd forgotten to bring home a bed for him.

'I'm sorry, boy,' I said, 'this isn't a very good start, is it?'

I looked around for a makeshift bed for him but there was nothing. I thought for a while. *Got it!* I ran into my bedroom, pulled out a drawer from my large chest of drawers and tipped out all the jumpers. Then I grabbed a blanket from my cupboard and folded it up so it would fit inside. Finally, I placed Gus's teddy bear and my soft toy elephant in it to keep him company. I carried his new sleeping quarters into the living room to show him.

'*Ta-da!*' I said, enthusiastically putting the drawer down. 'What do you think?'

He looked at me as if to say, *it's a drawer*. Perhaps he didn't know it was meant for him to sleep in? Yes, that was it; he needed me to show him. I squeezed myself in as best I could and lay down.

'Come on, boy,' I said, getting out. 'Your turn.' And I patted the blanketed drawer. He breathed a heavy sigh, got off my coat and trudged over to his new bed. 'I heard that,' I said.

Gus got into his new bed, which couldn't have been too uncomfortable, because he lay down, put his head on the elephant and instantly fell asleep.

He was dog-tired. I don't think he'd slept much in the kennels, what with all the other dogs barking, the constant clanging of metal food bowls and the draughts. He was making up for it now though.

As Gus slept, I watched my new dog twitching

away. He was dreaming and his paws were moving fast, as though he was running. Was he chasing cats like most normal dogs or was he running away from the police?

Later, while I was still trying to figure it out, as I watched some telly, I became aware of a strange noise. I'd lived in that flat for a whole year and had never heard it before. It sounded a bit like my upstairs neighbour hoovering but it couldn't be; he was away on holiday.

I turned the volume down in case it was coming from the TV, but the noise continued. What on earth could it be? I listened harder. It was getting louder. I crept into the bedroom; no, it wasn't coming from in there. I crept into the bathroom; nothing. Perhaps it was the fridge humming? I checked the kitchen, but the fridge was as quiet as the cheese inside it.

I followed the trail of sound until I found where it was coming from. *Uh-oh!* It was coming from the elderly black mongrel asleep in the drawer. *Oh, great! My new dog snores!!!*

He even woke himself up after one particularly loud snore.

It had been a big day for both Gus and me, so I turned off the telly and took him out for his last wee of the night. We came back and flopped into bed; me into my bed and Gus into his drawer.

I was woken up by what sounded like a herd of buffaloes in my living room. I opened one eye and looked at my watch – I'd only been asleep for twenty minutes! What was going on??? I grabbed my tennis racket in case it was a burglar (who fancied a game) and crept through the flat. I slowly peeked round the living-room door.

I saw a black dog with a pink elephant in his mouth, flinging it up in the air and catching it! Ah, now I got it – I was dreaming. Hang on a minute; no, I wasn't. This was real – I *really* had brought Gus home to live with me, it *really* was half-past midnight and there *really* was a supposedly very sick dog in my living room – who was having the time of his life!

'Oi,' I said, my elephant in mid-air, 'I thought you were meant to be seriously ill.' The elephant landed just in front of Gus, who decided it was a danger to us both and needed to be dealt with. First he pulled one of its back legs off, then its left ear, and finally he yanked its head off. He looked at me rather pleased as if to say, *I've saved us, we can go back to sleep now.* Gus, I *was* asleep!

We got back into our beds and I fell asleep again, but this time I was woken up by a loud slurping noise. *What now???* I dragged myself out of bed to investigate. It was 2 a.m. and Gus was drinking out of the toilet.

'Why?' I asked him, almost crying now. 'Why, when you've got a perfectly good bowl of *clean* water in the kitchen, would you drink out of the toilet?' There was only one way to deal with this. I put the toilet lid down, got back into bed, wondering if dog-owners ever got any sleep, and shoved some earplugs into my ears.

The earplugs worked a treat; almost too well, because I fell into a deep sleep. I dreamed I was introducing Gus to my family – his new relatives. The dream turned out to be more of a nightmare with Gus peeing on my mum's expensive rug, chewing my brother's mobile phone and digging up my dad's nearly finished 1000-piece jigsaw, which was carefully laid out on the spare-room floor.

I woke up with a start. Phew; thank goodness it was just a dream. I knew why I'd had that dream though; I was anxious about my family meeting Gus. They weren't exactly dog-lovers, which was strange because I loved dogs so much.

I knew I wasn't adopted, but perhaps there had been a mix-up in the hospital when I was born? It seemed far more likely that my real parents lived on a farm somewhere with forty dogs and a child that wasn't theirs.

I was exhausted, but at least it was the weekend which meant I didn't have to get up straight away; I could have a nice long lie-in. Oh no, I couldn't! As soon as I opened my eyes Gus came into focus. He was standing over me, his nose almost touching mine, with a rather desperate look on his face. I quickly realized he was busting for a wee – or a poo. It didn't matter; the point was, if I wanted to save my carpets, *we had to get out of there – RIGHT NOW*!

I threw on some clothes, ignoring the fact that I too needed to wee, and we raced to the park. We were just in time. As soon as we got there Gus ran like a champion sprinter straight into the bushes. The minute he was done we had to race back home so I could go! And that was when I saw my flat properly for the first time that morning. My mouth fell open as I surveyed the wreckage before me.

Gus had obviously decided the drawer was not for him last night, because my cream-coloured spotlessly clean sofa was now black, hairy and decidedly doggy. My cuddly pink elephant was now not just in four pieces but twenty-four. Most of my precious pristine plants had snot hanging from their leaves, and the TV remote control had been chewed.

'GUS!' I yelled. 'Gus, get your furry backside in here!'

Thinking it was banana time, he happily trotted in and sat at my feet.

'Right,' I said, looking down at my raggedy lifelong dream, 'if you and I are going to live together, there are going to have to be a few rules. There will be *no* . . .

- drinking from the toilet
- sleeping on the sofa
- chewing my property – I will get you your own property to chew
- snotting on the plants
- eating the remote control . . .

★

'Understand?'

I must have been boring him, because he yawned the world's biggest yawn, giving me an eyeful of those manky brown teeth and a noseful of that appalling dog breath.

'And we *absolutely must* get your bad breath under control!'

CHAPTER FOUR

A Mongrel Makeover

The next four weeks came and went in a flash. Gus's coughing and sneezing ceased and he was beginning to resemble a healthy, happy hound. He'd put on some weight and was now a little heavier – unlike my bank balance, which was definitely a whole lot lighter.

I was learning fast that having a dog wasn't cheap. He needed a lot of new stuff:

- a brand-new collar and lead

- a comfy new bed and blanket
- toys
- food
- a waterproof coat
- a brush
- a new food bowl
- a new water bowl

But I couldn't afford to get everything all at once. I worked out I could buy four things today; the other four, I'd have to come back for next week. Which four do you think were the most important things to get?

We bought the stuff home and collapsed, exhausted. I took Gus's brand-new blue-and-white spotted lead and collar off, packed away his food, placed his new bed and blanket in the living room and put his waterproof coat in a drawer.

As Gus snored from his new bed (I think he liked it!), I knew I couldn't put it off any longer. I picked up the phone and dialled my parents' number; it was high time my family met their new four-legged relative.

Ring ring.

They'll disown me.

Ring ring.

They'll never want to come for tea again.

Ring ring.

I'll never be invited for Sunday lunch.

Ring ring.

How would my mum react to the news that her first grandchild was a dog? Not very well, I'd imagine.

'Hello?' It was my mum.

'Oh hi, Mum,' I said. 'Erm, what are you doing on Sunday?'

'Nothing. Why?' she replied.

'There's someone I'd like you to meet. I'll bring him round about tea time.'

There, I'd done it; well, sort of. I'd chickened out of telling them that for the first time in our history we had a dog in the family, but at least I'd arranged for them to meet.

'Right, Gus,' I said to my stinky hound,

'if you're going to meet your human granny and granddad, you'll have to be at your shiny, sparkling best. Today is Tuesday; we have five days to transform you.'

Gus snored another foghorn snore. I could tell he was excited.

Some dogs are bath-lovers and some are bath-haters, and not having had Gus for very long I wasn't quite sure which he was. Oh well, if we were going to wash away the last of that nasty kennel smell and make Gus presentable enough to meet my mum, there was only one way to find out.

'Gus,' I called from the bathroom.

Nothing.

'Gus, come here, boy.'

Nothing.

He must have heard the shower going and decided that being called towards it could only mean one thing: he was going under it. I went to get him, but he wasn't in the living room. I looked in the kitchen; no Gus. He must be in my bedroom; strange, he wasn't in there either. He definitely wasn't in the bathroom because I'd just come from there. This was very odd; he can't have just disappeared.

I looked again and found him wedged under my bed. Gus was definitely a bath-hater! This was going to be fun.

I lay flat on my tummy and reached under the bed. If I stretched as far as I possibly could, I could just about reach his collar. I hooked my fingers through it and pulled with all my might.

Slowly but surely, like a cork inching out of a bottle, Gus was almost out.

'Nearly there . . . just a little more . . .' And just when I thought he was going to pop out, he dipped his head, slipped his collar and reversed back under the bed.

'OK,' I said to him, 'if that's the way you want it, two can play at that game.' I left him under the bed and went into the kitchen. At a time like this, only one thing would do – I reached for a banana.

Back in the bedroom, I got on my hands and knees and waved half the banana under his nose. He shuffled forward a little way and took it. I broke off some small bits from the other half and made a trail all the way from Gus's nose to the hallway. I hid behind the door ready to pounce when he was close enough. He came out as far as the edge of the bed and even though I knew he really wanted the rest of the banana, he obviously didn't want it enough to risk a bath. For once, the magic banana had failed me.

I had one more trick up my sleeve. I picked up my keys, put on my coat, grabbed Gus's lead and opened the front door.

'*Walkies!*' I said in my best sing-song voice. It worked; Gus shot out from under the bed and darted to the front door where I was waiting for him. I scooped him up, which wasn't easy as he'd put on some weight, kicked the front door shut and ran him into the bath.

The showerhead was in the bath, still running with warm water. I held onto a very squirmy

Gus with one hand and wet him all over with the other. He looked up at me with a long-suffering look on his face.

'Oh, it's not so bad,' I said to him. 'At least it's warm. And I'm about to give you a lovely massage with this' – I held the shampoo bottle up to my eyes – 'special strawberry dog shampoo.' I must say, it did smell good.

I poured some over Gus's back and, with the hand I wasn't using to hold him still, began to massage it in. His coat was very thick, and to make sure I got it all over him I had to use both hands. I don't think he liked strawberries, because just then he began an almighty shake, as though he was doing some sort of strange dog dance. It started up in his ears, went all the way down his body and ended right at the tip of his tail, with pink watery soapsuds flicking out in every direction.

I felt as though I'd had a pink foam custard pie thrown in my face and fell backwards, trying to wipe it out of my hair, face and eyes. Gus must have realized this was his chance to escape, because before I knew what was happening he'd leaped out of the bath and was running all over the flat, shaking himself everywhere!

He jumped on my bed, rolling around on the white duvet and turning it a sloppy wet shade of pink. I tried to grab him, but he was too quick. He flew off the bed and into the living room, shaking shampoo all over my sofa, all over the TV and all over the table. As he ran towards the kitchen I lunged and caught him – but he was as slippery as a seal and escaped once more.

When he'd shaken as much water from his coat as he could, he began wiping his body all over the carpet. He was lying on his side, using his back legs to propel himself around the flat at breakneck speed! I'd never seen anything like it before.

'Have you quite finished?' I asked him when he'd stopped scooting around the flat. By now I wasn't sure which was hairier: Gus, or my beige (now hairy and black) carpet. He snorted, which I took to mean he had.

I still had to get the shampoo out of his coat;

how on earth was I going to do this? I'd never get him back in the bath now. I looked outside. It was pouring with rain. A smile crawled across my face. I put on my wellies and a full-length raincoat, flipped up the hood and once again sang at the top of my voice, '*Walkies!*'

Gus had been tricked once before in this way and he hesitated. But when he saw me walking out the front door he realized it wasn't a trick this time.

Gus and I trudged round the block five times. The first two times, he left a pink soapy trail of bubbles and foam behind him. After the third the water ran clear, but we walked round twice more just to be sure.

'You look like you've just been pulled out of the river Thames,' I said as I began towel-drying my sopping wet dog. His cold and cough had completely gone, but I didn't want them to come back so, just to be sure, I got the hairdryer out. I sat on the floor and put it on the lowest setting in case it frightened him.

I needn't have worried; he loved it! As soon as his front had dried, he turned his side to the warm, comforting breeze. As soon as his side was dry he turned his back to it. And as soon as his back was dry he turned his last damp side towards the hairdryer. When he was completely dry I turned it off.

'Did you like that, boy?' I asked. I looked at my newly clean, fluffy dog – was that a smile I could see on his face? Gus burrowed his nose under my hand. 'You want a stroke?' I asked him. He wanted more than that, and plonked his strawberry-smelling self right in my lap! He was a bit of a heavy lump, but he was *my* heavy lump and I gave him the biggest cuddle ever.

Gus's makeover was nearly complete but we still had one big problem to sort out and we had to do it by Sunday. Gus's dog breath still smelled like old fishy trainers.

Some people brush their dog's teeth using a special doggy toothbrush and toothpaste.

Judging by the trouble I'd had trying to squirt cough medicine into Gus's mouth, I knew this would never work. And besides, Gus's teeth were way beyond brushing.

There was only one thing for it. I picked up the phone and called the dog dentist. Two days later we were sitting in the vet's waiting room. The office door flew open and out came the vet. It was that same old deaf vet who'd looked after Gus in the kennels.

'Buzz,' he called to the waiting patients. There were three other people waiting; one had a cat, one had a snake and the other had a parrot in a cage.

'Buzz?' he repeated, looking over the top of his glasses when no one got up. We all looked at each other and then it suddenly dawned on me; he meant Gus. I jumped up out of my seat. The other people must have thought I was a bit strange, forgetting my own dog's name!

Once inside the vet's office I lifted Gus onto the examination table.

'My word, Buzz,' said the friendly old vet, 'you look like a brand-new dog. The last time I saw you, you were feeling very sorry for yourself.'

He looked into Gus's eyes, in his ears and up his nose. He took out his stethoscope and listened to Gus's heart. I knew his cough and cold had gone and I was half hoping his heart murmur might have gone too, but I knew this was wishful thinking.

'Aside from his heart murmur, his chest and lungs are all clear,' the vet said to me. 'Well done, you've done a splendid job.' He opened Gus's mouth for a quick look. 'Phew! What a stink!'

'I know, that's why we're here,' I said. 'I think Gus is going to need a dental.'

'What?' said the vet, straining to hear me. 'You think he's going mental?' His hearing hadn't improved.

'No, HE NEEDS A DENTAL!' I yelled in his ear.

'I see,' he said, and took a closer look at Gus's molars. 'Some of them are rotten; that'll be the smell and the rest are in a pretty awful state. You realize we'll need to take some out, don't you?'

Good, I thought. Not only would that get the smell under control, but it might also stop him chewing up my remote control!

The vet had a good old rummage around inside Gus's mouth. He might have been deaf, that old vet, but he was *very* brave. 'Sorting out Gus's mouth is going to be quite a big job, you know,' he said. 'We're going to have to knock him out with a general anaesthetic.'

I had expected this.

The vet continued, 'I have to explain something to you,' he said, looking rather serious. 'All anaesthetics carry a risk, but especially so in Gus's case because of his bad heart.'

Oh, I hadn't thought about that. Suddenly I wasn't so sure he needed a dental after all. 'Perhaps we should leave his teeth as they are,' I said, 'or I could just start brushing them?' As

I said this I had visions of the toothpaste ending up all over the walls and in my hair instead of in Gus's mouth.

The vet shook his head and said, 'It's too late for that. His teeth are so rotten they'll end up poisoning him. We really have no choice.'

I was suddenly feeling very nervous.

'I can do Gus's dental tomorrow, but it's very important he has an empty stomach,' said the vet. 'Make sure he doesn't eat anything after six o'clock tonight and take his water bowl away just before you go to bed. Any food or water in his stomach might make him sick while he's under the anaesthetic and that would be very bad. Got it?'

'Got it,' I said, writing down all the instructions just in case. 'See you tomorrow,' I said to the vet.

'Eh? What is it you need to borrow?' he asked.

'No, nothing, never mind,' and with that Gus and I left.

★

At 5.30 that evening, I gave Gus his favourite food – not steak, sausages or chicken, which would be most dogs' favourite food, but fruit salad. What a strange dog I had!

For the rest of that evening I just stared at Gus, worrying myself to death. I'd only had him for a month, but now I couldn't imagine life without him. In such a short space of time he'd wormed his way right into my heart. We did everything together and he and I had become best friends. Tomorrow he was going to have an anaesthetic. Would his heart survive it?

Before getting into bed I took his water away and I made absolutely sure the toilet lid was shut!

The next morning Gus and I arrived at the vet's bright and early.

'You will take extra good care of him, won't you?' I said to the veterinary nurse. 'You know his heart's a bit wonky.'

'Of course we will,' she replied. 'You can

73

pick him up at four-thirty this afternoon. He'll be a bit woozy but he can still go home.'

This made me feel better, although I couldn't concentrate on anything that day:

People spoke to me but I didn't hear them.

I bought some shopping but left half the bags behind.

I parked on a yellow line and didn't even notice the ticket on my windscreen.

And all day long I put things down and forgot to pick them up again . . .

Luckily I didn't forget to pick Gus up and I was at the vet's half an hour early.

'You're early,' said the receptionist.

'How is he?' I asked eagerly.

'You'll have to speak to the vet,' she said.

My heart sank. Something must have gone wrong. 'What's happened? Is he dead? He's dead, isn't he? Was it his heart? It was his heart, wasn't it? You can tell me, I can take it, *please just tell me!*'

'Calm down,' the receptionist said. 'I don't

know how he is – I just book the appointments and make the tea.'

'Oh. Sorry.' I was a little embarrassed by my outburst. I took a seat and watched the clock, my left leg constantly jiggling with nerves. Twenty minutes later the vet came out. Behind his white beard and bushy eyebrows it was hard to tell if he was looking happy or sad. Gus wasn't with him. I felt sick.

And then, ever so slowly and walking a little wobbly, out came Gus, my favourite boy in the whole wide world. My heart almost burst with joy when I saw him. He looked a little drunk and swayed around as though he was dancing on ice, but the most important thing was he'd made it – he'd survived the anaesthetic!

When he saw me he swayed faster in my direction, his tail wagging like mad.

'Well,' said the vet, 'as you can see, he's fine. He's a bit woozy because he's just come round from a deep sleep. Take him home and let him sleep it off and he'll be as right as rain in the morning.'

I was so happy I gave Gus a big kiss on his furry white face, and then I gave the vet a big kiss on *his* furry white face too. I scooped Gus up in my arms and squeezed him tight. He made a funny noise that sounded like a cow mooing.

'Wanna go home, boy?' I asked.

He wagged his tail and licked my face. And that was when it hit me: no more death breath! I put Gus back down on the floor and gently opened up his mouth. His breath smelled sweet, like a puppy's, and there were no more rotten teeth. Hang on a minute – there were hardly any teeth at all!

I looked up at the vet.

'Erm, yes,' he said, 'we had to take out rather more than I'd bargained for.'

Poor Gus only had four teeth left in his whole head, which isn't many considering dogs normally have forty-two!

Lucky he liked squashy banana!

CHAPTER FIVE

Gus meets his Family

'Now remember, Gus,' I said, looking down at my sparkling clean dog, 'don't pee on the carpet, don't chew any mobile phones, and if you see a nearly-finished jigsaw puzzle on the floor don't go anywhere near it.' He looked up at me, panting, and the glorious smell of fresh breath wafted up towards me. Thank goodness we'd sorted that stinky little problem out before Gus met the family!

He looked very handsome in his blue-and-white spotted collar with matching lead. My mum would approve – she liked things that matched.

I rang the doorbell. My mum opened the door. She was done up like a dog's dinner. Gus must have thought so too because he jumped straight up at her, wagging his tail. His claws got caught in her dress and tore it. My mum screamed, frightening Gus half to death, and he bolted inside the flat to where my dad and brother were lying on the ground doing the same thousand-piece jigsaw I'd seen in my dream.

'Gus!' I yelled. '*No!*'

My dad, who was also dressed unusually smartly, jumped up as soon as he saw me. 'What's going on?' he said, looking more than a little confused. 'Who's this?'

My mum was hurrying into the living room holding her dress up as best she could.

'Mum, Dad, Marcus . . . this is Gus.'

My brother burst out laughing.

'What's so funny?' I asked. Now I was confused.

'Mum and Dad thought you were bringing a new boyfriend over!' my brother said. 'That's why they're all dressed up!'

'Oh, Mum, I'm so sorry, I should have said. And I'm sorry about your dress.'

My mum didn't answer. She just stood there opening and closing her mouth. She reminded me of Horace, one of our many family goldfish.

'What exactly is he?' asked my dad, looking at Gus as though he were an alien from another planet.

'A dog,' I replied.

'Don't be cheeky!' he said. 'I know he's a dog, but what sort of dog is he?'

'A good dog,' I said, and Gus wagged his tail as though in agreement. 'He's got a bit of husky in him, I think.'

'That'll be handy if it snows,' said my brother. 'I think we've still got the old toboggan!'

'Is he housetrained?' asked my mum. 'Does he bite?' I couldn't tell if the look on her face was one of horror or terror.

'Yes and no,' I replied confidently.

We had a rather awkward sit-down tea, with Gus choosing to sit next to my mother and drool over her shoes while she ate her cake. When Gus farted I thought it was probably time to leave. I scoffed my cake, gulped my tea, and we made our excuses and left.

On the drive home, I looked at my floppy-eared dog in the rear-view mirror. 'Well, boy,' I said, 'it's true what they say: you can choose your friends, but you can't choose your family! I know they're not very doggy, but we're stuck with them. Perhaps you can change their minds and make them see how brilliant dogs are.' He let out a sigh and lay down. 'No,' I agreed, 'I'm not sure you can either, but let's give it a go, shall we?

Over the next few months, Gus and I discovered many things about each other.

I discovered that Gus:

- hated baths but loved the hairdryer

- loved fruit salad, especially bananas
- was perfectly housetrained
- was scared of thunderstorms
- was terrified of spiders
- liked cats and loved dogs
- howled at the *EastEnders* theme tune (causing me great embarrassment eight times a week)

Gus discovered that I:

- loved baths and loved the hairdryer
- hated fruit salad
- was perfectly housetrained
- was scared of thunderstorms
- was terrified of spiders
- liked cats and loved dogs
- howled whenever he chewed my things (causing Gus great embarrassment twenty times a week)

All of these discoveries were perfectly

manageable except for one – thunderstorms. Sometimes Gus would just sit and stare out of the window. I wondered what he was looking at and then it dawned on me; he was watching the weather. If more than a few dark storm clouds gathered, Gus would start to shake and drool. That's when I knew it was time to close the curtains!

By now Gus had made many four-legged friends in our local park, and with his new fresher breath he was attracting many more. Before his dental, he'd bound up to other dogs but they'd usually shrink away from his wheelie-bin breath. Things were definitely looking up now though, and Gus had even managed to find himself a girlfriend. Her name was Sally and she was a beautiful honey-coloured golden retriever.

Sally wasn't a rescue dog like Gus; she was a posh, pretty pedigree dog and had cost Mrs Bridgewater, her owner, an absolute fortune. And it showed. Her golden coat shone like the sun, her brown eyes were bright and keen, and her diamond collar dazzled in the daylight. Her breath smelled like a summer breeze, so it was quite fitting that the two freshest-breath dogs in the park should fall head over heels in love, just like *Lady and the Tramp*.

The very tall and elegant Mrs Bridgewater was horrified that her prize pedigree should fancy an elderly mongrel with a dodgy heart who only had four teeth.

'Sally!' Mrs Bridgewater called, waving a roast-beef-flavoured treat at her dog. 'Sally, come away.' But Sally was smitten with Gus, and no amount of coaxing or tasty treats could drag her away. In desperation Mrs Bridgewater threw the treat to Sally – only to see Gus helpfully hoover it up!

Sally lived with a ferret called Humphrey, whose collar matched hers, and wherever Sally went Humphrey followed. Gus wasn't quite sure what to make of Humphrey. Perhaps he thought Humphrey was a long, short cat. But it didn't really matter what he was; any friend of Sally's was a friend of Gus's.

Sally and Gus cavorted around the park, chasing each other and rolling around on the grass. Mrs Bridgewater joined in the chase, doing her very best to keep the two dogs apart and Humphrey followed behind, doing his very best to keep up!

I spotted another of Gus's friends bounding over for a play. 'Morning, Dusty,' I said, bending down to stroke the small Weetabix-coloured terrier, 'how's life?'

She wagged her tail hard, which I took to mean 'good'.

Just like Gus, Dusty the Border terrier was a rescue dog. She was a stray and her owner never came to claim her. Luckily Val was there to give Dusty a good *new* home. When Val and Dusty's eyes met through the kennel bars it was love at first sight. Both were small, both had brown eyes and both had the same colour hair!

Gus saw Dusty, and came speeding over with Sally in tow.

'Sally!' yelled Mrs Bridgewater once again. *'Sally, will you come here!'* Sally looked over to her owner, but decided that the choice between a cross-looking mistress and her furry fun-loving boyfriend was an easy one to make.

'That's right, Sally,' whispered Val, patting the golden retriever. 'You stay here with us and have some fun.'

They were having so much fun that Gus hadn't noticed the storm clouds gathering, and from nowhere came a sudden and deafening crack of thunder. Three humans, three dogs and a ferret all jumped in the air – but no one jumped higher than Gus. Terrified, he bolted and began running blindly, straight for the lake.

'GGGUUUUUSSSSS!' I yelled, but I knew he couldn't hear me. Lightning flashed across the sky and the thunder boomed as the storm moved closer. More lightning split the clouds –

Gus saw it too and, never taking his eyes off the angry sky above, just kept running.

He ran straight through the barriers put up around the lake to stop people getting too close. A mudslide had caused one of the banks to fall away, creating a steep drop into the water below. Gus was running at full speed and couldn't stop himself in time, but as fast as he was going it all seemed to happen in slow motion.

I ran as fast as I could, and when I reached the bank I peered down, waiting for his head to pop up out of the water. I counted the seconds: *six . . . seven . . . eight . . . where was he?*

'Gus?' I began to panic. '*Gus!*' Gus loved splashing around in water, but in all the time I'd had him I'd never once seen him go out of his depth. Even when I threw a stick far out for him he'd let it go, preferring to feel some watery ground beneath his paws. Did this mean he couldn't swim?

Mrs Bridgewater was next to reach the bank.

'I saw what happened,' she said, looking down. 'Where is he?'

'I don't know,' I replied, my voice shaking. 'He hasn't come up yet.'

Ten . . . eleven . . . twelve . . .

'Here.' I turned round and threw my coat at her. It landed on Humphrey, and she just managed to hang onto both coat and ferret. She raised an eyebrow and said, 'You're not going in there, are you?'

Val finally reached the lake, huffing and puffing. 'What are you doing?' she said, open-mouthed. 'You can't go in there!' She was staring at me as though I'd lost my marbles. Dusty was anxiously dancing around at Val's feet, and Sally – Gus's golden girlfriend – was barking her head off.

'Sally, no!' said Mrs Bridgewater, and grabbed her dog just as she was about to leap in after Gus. 'One dog in there is quite enough, thank you very much.'

Fifteen . . . sixteen . . .

'I have to save him,' I said, and flung my shoes at Val. I prepared to dive and then thought better of it; I didn't know how deep, or shallow, it was. Instead of a dive I opted for the safety of the dive bomb – not quite as elegant, but less chance of me breaking my neck.

'Sorry, Mrs B!' I shouted behind me as the aftermath of my dive bomb soaked her.

I knew it was going to be cold, but I couldn't have imagined just how f . . . f . . . freezing it would really be. Under the water, everything went cold, quiet and numb. I surfaced with green weed and duck poo clinging to my head. The surrounding ducks had flapped their wings and made a run for it. But I still couldn't see Gus. Where on earth was he?

'GUUUSSS!' I swam out a little further so that I could see the whole lake from the middle. Still no sign.

A crowd of onlookers had gathered next to Mrs Bridgewater. 'Can you see him?' she yelled.

'No, can you?' I shouted back. She shook her head. I swam back to where Gus had fallen in and dived down in case he'd got trapped under the water. I couldn't see a thing so I felt my way around. Eek, what was that? It felt like an eel. And was that a . . . a supermarket trolley? Yes, and I could feel an old bicycle too.

I felt around some more. Sludge, a tyre, more sludge – but there was nothing Gus-shaped. I was running out of breath, mainly because I was panicking. I could feel myself beginning to cry. Gus had drowned; I just knew it.

I surfaced, turning away from Val and Mrs Bridgewater because I wanted to compose myself before I faced them and the awful truth. I wiped the sludge and the tears from my eyes. I was so upset I couldn't even feel the cold any more.

I turned round and saw Mrs Bridgewater and Val standing on the bank at the water's edge, waving at me. On one side of them Sally sat perfectly still and perfectly upright, watching my every move. On the other side of them, Dusty lay quietly. And in the middle, hopping around on the spot and barking his head off, was an elderly black mongrel with a grey face and pointed ears that flopped over at the ends!

Was I seeing things? Was I going mad? Had I swallowed too much duck poo? I wiped my eyes again, but there was no mistake; it was my boy. I swam towards the three of them, hauled myself out of the water and dragged myself up the steep bank. The storm had moved on and it was no longer raining, but my clothes were heavy with water and the cold had taken my breath away.

'Gus!' I gasped and gave him the biggest squeeze. He made a sound like a bagpipe. 'Where *were* you?' He looked up at me, bewildered. I took off my jumper and wrung it out. Mrs Bridgewater put my dry coat round me. Suddenly I was freezing cold and my teeth began chattering. 'D-don't ever d-do that to m-me again,' I said, shivering. 'D-do you h-hear me?'

Gus sneezed, and then ran off to play with his girlfriend as though nothing had happened!

'I don't understand why you threw yourself in,' said Mrs Bridgewater. 'Everyone knows that all dogs can swim.'

'But G-Gus isn't all d-dogs,' I replied.

'You're not wrong!' said Mrs Bridgewater. 'He really is quite unique.'

Hmm, that was certainly one way of putting it!

CHAPTER SIX

Gus Goes to School

'Does your dog bite?' asked the lady sitting next to me on the park bench. Her ten-year-old daughter sat right at the very end, as far away from Gus as possible, looking warily at him. She had long blonde hair and wore a bright red coat.

'I'd like to see him try,' I laughed. 'He's only got four teeth!'

'Four teeth?' said the girl, suddenly interested. 'How come he's only got four?'

'Well,' I replied, 'his teeth were so rotten that the vet had to pull most of them out. Good job too; you should have smelled his breath beforehand – *phee-ew*!'

'What's his name?' asked the girl, smiling.

'It's Gus,' I replied. 'What's yours?'

'Sasha. And I don't like dogs.'

'You and my mum would get on well,' I said. 'Why don't you like dogs?' I asked. 'What's not to like?'

'She was bitten by a dog a few months ago,' Sasha's mum explained, 'and now she won't go near them.'

Sasha was staring at Gus, who was sunbathing with his head on my shoes. He snored the biggest snore, making Sasha guffaw with laughter.

'I've never heard a dog snore before!' she giggled.

'This is nothing,' I said. 'You should hear him in the middle of the night – he sounds like an old pig grunting!' That made her laugh even more.

'Can I stroke him?' asked Sasha's mum.

'Of course you can,' I replied. 'He's *very* friendly.'

Sasha's mum bent down to stroke Gus, who began wagging his tail in his sleep. 'I think that's where we went wrong before, with the dog that bit Sasha,' she said. 'You see, we didn't ask his owner if we could stroke him and he obviously wasn't as friendly as Gus.'

By now, Sasha had shuffled along towards the middle of the bench and was watching her mum stroke Gus. I could tell she wanted to stroke him too, but because of what had happened to her she couldn't quite pluck up the courage. I decided to help things along a little. I didn't want this poor girl to go through life always being scared of dogs; that simply wouldn't do. I thought I'd begin by telling Sasha a bit about Gus.

'I haven't always had him, you know,' I said to her. 'Even though he's quite old, I've only had him for a year and a half. He's a rescue dog.'

'What's that?' she asked.

'Well, his owner was sent to prison and Gus ended up in a dogs' home,' I said. 'He was in a terrible way – sad, lonely and very sick – so I rescued him and brought him home to live with me.'

'How old is he?' Sasha asked.

'Not sure,' I replied, 'but I know he's old because the fur around his face has gone all grey and white, just like people's hair goes grey and white when they get old. Another way you can tell a dog's age is by looking at his teeth. Gus's were awful, all manky and brown before the vet pulled them out; that's a sure sign he's old. I think he's going a bit deaf too.'

'He sounds just like my granddad!' Sasha said, grinning.

'Well,' I continued, 'if Gus was human he'd probably be about the same age as your granddad.' Her eyes widened. 'I think you should look upon Gus as a doggy version of him.' This did the trick.

'Can I stroke him?' she asked.

'I think he'd love that,' I replied. 'Gus, wakey wakey, there's someone here who wants to meet you,' I said. At the mention of his name, Gus lifted his head from my shoes. He stood up, stretched and yawned a long chewy yawn. His pink tongue curled up at the end of his yawn. Just to make sure he was properly awake, he shook himself from the tip of his nose all the way down to the tip of his tail.

Very slowly he walked over to Sasha and sat down next to her. She looked over to her mum and me.

'Where should I stroke him first?' she asked.

'On his chest,' I said. 'Gus is super-friendly and would love you to stroke him just about anywhere, but some dogs get a little worried when you put your hand over their head to pat them, especially if they've been mistreated before – they might think you're going to hit them. It's always best to start by stroking a dog gently on its chest.'

Sasha slowly took her hand out of her pocket and reached for Gus's chest. Gus sniffed her hand just in case there might be a treat coming his way.

'That's it,' I said. 'Let him sniff your hand first.'

Gus's sniff over with, Sasha gently placed her hand on Gus's chest. 'His fur is very thick,' she said as her hand disappeared into his deep, luxuriant coat.

'I think that's because one of his parents was a husky,' I said, 'and huskies were used for pulling sleds in a freezing cold, snowy place called Siberia. They wouldn't have got very far if they didn't have thick fur coats to keep out the icy cold!'

'It feels lovely,' Sasha said, mesmerized by the feel of Gus's fur. 'Look, his tail's wagging!'

'I tell you what'll make it wag even more,' I replied. 'Give him a scratch behind one of his ears.'

Sasha was fascinated by Gus's ears; the way

they stood up but then flopped over at the tips. She scratched behind his right ear. Both Gus and Sasha were in heaven, and when he put his head on her lap she squealed with delight (quietly, so as not to startle him).

I handed her a packet of treats. 'Want to feed him one?' I asked. She wasn't so sure about this because it meant going near Gus's mouth – and to Sasha, a dog's mouth meant one thing: teeth!

'Go on,' I said. 'He's only got four teeth. What's the worse he could do – gum you?!'

Sasha and her mum started laughing. Sasha pulled a treat out of the packet and handed it to Gus, who took it ever so gently from her. He lay down on the ground to eat it – quite right too; you have to be comfortable to properly enjoy a roast-beef-flavoured treat!

'Thank you so much,' Sasha's mum said. 'I couldn't bear Sasha going through life being scared of dogs.'

'Well, we're here in the park at this time

every day,' I said, 'so hopefully we'll see you and Sasha again soon.'

We did see them again. It was a week later, but this time it was for more than just a pat.

'Gu-us!' yelled a voice in the distance. I wasn't sure who it was, but then I saw Sasha's bright red coat. Being a little deaf, Gus took a bit longer to hear her, but when he did he bounded over to her.

'Hello, boy,' she said, kneeling down to stroke him. She hadn't forgotten what I'd said and let him sniff her hand before reaching for his chest.

'I'm so glad we've seen you,' said Sasha's mum. 'I was telling some of the other mums at school about how Gus helped Sasha overcome her fear of dogs and they all thought it'd be a brilliant idea if you and Gus went along and gave a talk to Sasha's class.'

'Me? Give a talk?' I said, feeling sick at the very thought of it.

'Oh, please,' Sasha begged. 'Some of my class are scared of dogs too and Gus could help them the same way he helped me.' They were both kneeling down and stroking Gus, who was loving all the attention.

'Anyway,' continued Sasha's mum, 'a few of us spoke to Miss Bailey, Sasha's teacher, and she was hoping you and Gus might come into school one afternoon next week. She said her class would love to meet Gus, and he's so gentle even the kids who are frightened of dogs would see just how lovely dogs really are.'

Well, I agreed with her about that, and I knew that Gus would be the perfect ambassador for his species. If I could show just one child that dogs were utterly brilliant it'd be worth it. But I was terrified of speaking to groups of people. My mouth went all dry and I stumbled over my words. Half of me was saying, *Go on, do it*, but the other half was saying, *Don't!* What would you have done?

'OK, we'd love to,' I said. 'Just tell me when

and where and we'll be there!' That was one of the wonderful things about having a dog; I wasn't an '*I*' any more, I was a '*we*'.

Two weeks later Gus and I filed in through the school gates. I hadn't been back inside a school since my very own school days and I was a bit nervous. It felt like my first day of school all over again!

I'd bought Gus a brand-new collar for this special occasion. It was bright red and looked stunning next to his shiny black coat. It had a matching lead, which I held onto tightly.

I rang the bell and was buzzed in. Gus and I walked up the carpeted stairs to a large foyer with a corridor running through it and lots of closed doors on either side. The only open door was to an office that had a sign saying *School Secretary*. I knocked on the open door.

'Yes?' said a rather scary-looking lady from behind her desk. She had big black glasses, straight black hair and a wart on the end of her nose. If this was a film, she'd be the wicked witch and Gus would be the hero who'd come to save the children from her evil clutches. But this wasn't a film and the lady was tapping her pen on the desk, waiting for an answer.

'Erm,' I said, 'I, erm, we, erm, that is, me and my dog Gus are here to—'

'*Dog?*' said the lady, almost leaping over her desk. Her face changed from being frightening, fearsome and frowny to soft, sweet and smiley. 'I just *love* dogs! Where is he?'

'Down here,' I replied, pointing to Gus.

The lady stood up and peered over her desk. 'Hello, Gus,' she said.

Gus wasn't sure where the voice was coming from and looked all around him.

'Up here, boy,' I said, tapping on the desk. He looked up and wagged his tail at the school secretary. Just then the bell rang, all the doors were flung open and the whole area became a sea of green. Children in pea-coloured uniforms ran in every direction – that was, until they spied Gus.

'No way!' shouted one. 'There's a dog in school!'

'Wow! He's so cool!' yelled another.

'Miss, what's his name, miss?' I'd never been called 'miss' before and it took me a while to realize they were talking to me!

'Erm, it's Gus,' I said.

'Can we stroke him, miss?'

'Sure,' I replied, and about twelve small hands were suddenly all over Gus. I was feeling a little overwhelmed by all the attention, but Gus stood there taking it all in his stride, his tail swatting them in the face as he wagged with joy.

He licked one boy's face. 'Hey, did you see that,' the boy squealed to his friend. 'Gus just licked me!'

'That's disgusting,' said his friend, but then turned to Gus and said, 'Hey, Gus, lick me too!' Gus obliged and the boy was so chuffed he didn't even wipe Gus's slobber off!

'I'll tell you what's disgusting,' I said. 'If he'd done that to you before he went to the dog dentist, you'd be stinking like mouldy old cheese right now!'

'That's *gross*!' they all yelled.

'*What on earth is going on here?*' boomed a loud teacher-like voice. We all whizzed around to find a rather stout lady with frizzy red hair standing in front of us with her hands on her large hips. She wore glasses, a shirt done up all the way to the top, a brown skirt and sensible shoes. Everyone, including me, stopped talking and stood to attention. The children looked to me to explain.

'I'm h-here w-with my dog G-Gus to talk to Year S-six,' I said, my voice trembling.

'Right,' said the teacher, pointing to Gus and me. 'You two come with me; the rest of you have five seconds to get to your next lesson. *One . . . two . . .*' The children scattered in every direction. *They'll never make it*, I thought. '*. . . three . . . four . . .*' And to my amazement all but four of the kids had vanished. '*. . . five . . .*' And then those four disappeared too.

'Good trick,' I said to the teacher.

'*Hmmm*,' she said, looking over the top of her glasses at me. 'You want Miss Bailey's class. She's in that room over there.' She pointed to a purple door with a window in it.

I thanked her and Gus and I wandered over. Looking through the glass, I saw about twenty-five children sitting at their desks, facing the teacher. Some were fidgeting, others were staring out the window and some were just trying to stay awake. I remembered that feeling well. I knocked on the door and suddenly fifty eyes were on me, each and every one glad of the distraction.

'Come in,' sang Miss Bailey cheerily.

I opened the door, and immediately all eyes switched from me onto my furry four-legged friend.

'*Aaahhhh!*' hummed twenty-five voices all together; twenty-six with Miss Bailey's! Everyone was smiling. That was another thing I'd noticed since becoming a dog-owner; people around you smiled much more when you had a dog with you.

'*Gus!*' came a voice from the back. It was Sasha. Gus recognized her and wagged his tail hard as though saying hello right back.

'I hope you don't mind,' Miss Bailey said to me, 'but Sasha's done a special project about Gus, and she'd like to present it to the class.'

Mind? I was delighted someone else was taking charge! Sasha came up to the front of the class and knelt down to stroke her friend.

'I've always loved dogs,' Sasha began, 'but something happened a few months ago that made me really scared of them.' The class was silent and perfectly still, listening intently to her. 'There was this really cute little dog, all fluffy and white. It was so small and sweet that I bent down to stroke it.' No one in the class spoke and not one person fidgeted. Sasha continued, 'But then for no reason at all it suddenly bit me. I'm not sure why it did, as all I was doing was stroking it.'

Gus lay down on the floor with his head on Sasha's feet.

'That dog bit me twice on the hand and it was one of the most painful things ever. My mum had to take me to hospital for an injection so it wouldn't get infected.' Uneasy mumbles rumbled through the class. 'From that moment on I was terrified of dogs,' Sasha said. 'I hated them, and didn't want to be anywhere near them. My mum was really sad about this and kept telling me that most dogs were lovely. She tried showing me how friendly they were by stroking them in front of me. But I didn't want to know – that was, until I met Gus.'

At the mention of his name, Gus picked his head up.

'Gus was so gentle and handsome and friendly,' said Sasha, 'and I loved his ears! It was when I first met Gus and his owner that I learned two things. First, always ask the owner before stroking a dog I don't know. If I'd only done that with the little white dog, its owner would have told me not to and I wouldn't have been bitten. Second, if the owner says it's OK to stroke their dog, it's really important to always begin by letting the dog sniff your hand and then stroking it on its chest instead of its head so you don't frighten it.'

Sasha demonstrated on Gus who'd woken up and was now standing to attention next to Sasha. She asked him to sit, which he did. She then stroked him gently on his chest, moving her hand slowly up to his head so she could scratch him behind his ear. When she stopped, Gus nudged her hand for more and the whole class laughed. Finally she fed him a treat.

'Wow,' said a voice from the class. 'He's such a good dog!' To which Gus barked his approval and the whole class laughed once more.

'Thanks to Gus, I love dogs again,' said Sasha, 'and I'm really happy about that. It would have been horrible never to go near a dog again. Now I always stroke new ones I meet – after asking the owner's permission first, of course!'

Sasha went on to tell everyone all about Gus; how he was a rescue dog, that he only had four teeth and how much he loved bananas. When she'd finished, the class gave her an enthusiastic round of applause.

Not sure what was coming next, Miss Bailey and the rest of the class looked intently at me. Uh-oh, it was my turn now.

'Right,' I said, trying to sound like I knew what I was doing, 'who else would like to meet Gus?'

Twenty-five pairs of hands shot up in the air, but four of the children shook their heads.

'Why not?' I asked them.

'We're scared of dogs,' they replied.

'Gus isn't scary,' I said. 'He's got silly ears and only four teeth in his whole head. He's about as scary as Humpty Dumpty!' They giggled at this. 'OK,' I said, 'you don't have to meet him. We'll let the rest of the class come up and then see how you feel at the end.'

'*Single file!*' yelled Miss Bailey. '*And don't crowd Gus.*'

So one by one they all lined up to stroke Gus, with Miss Bailey at the front of the queue. After five whole minutes, the boy behind Miss Bailey said, 'Come on, miss, give the rest of us a go!' Miss Bailey reluctantly let go of Gus to give the boy behind a turn.

Gus adored all the attention and stood there wagging his tail as each child came up to pat him. They must have really been listening to Sasha's talk, because every single one of them began by letting Gus sniff their hand and then stroking him on his chest.

When everyone had had their turn patting Gus, they thanked me very much. 'You're welcome,' I said. 'Now, where are the four who didn't want to stroke Gus?' I asked.

'It was us, miss!' said the last four, who'd just been stroking Gus all over!

'Brilliant!' I said. 'But what changed your minds?'

'Seeing how gentle Gus was,' said one.

'I wanted to stroke his ears,' said another.

'I wanted to touch his bushy tail,' said the third.

'And I like his white whiskers,' said the fourth.

It didn't really matter what had changed their minds. The important thing was that they were no longer scared – Gus had shown them just how wonderful dogs truly are.

On our way home, I thought back to when I was at school. A lady from the Guide Dogs for the Blind had come and spoken to my class. She brought with her a young Labrador called Dillon who was having his Guide Dog training.

I fell in love with Dillon and did a project all about him and the Guide Dogs for the Blind. I got an A★. It was the only A★ I ever got, and I hoped our visit today had been just as memorable for Sasha and her class.

CHAPTER SEVEN

Gus and his Granny

'I must say . . .' my mum muttered, '. . . as dogs go, Gus is really quite an agreeable old soul, isn't he?' I was so shocked I nearly fell off my chair. This was progress, even though it had taken almost two years. If I wasn't very much mistaken, my mum was finally warming to her furry grandson.

'Yes,' I agreed, 'he is, isn't he.'

'Yes, he's a perfect four-legged gentleman – gentledog; you know what I mean.'

'Well, seeing as he's such a good boy, would you mind looking after him next Saturday afternoon?' I asked hopefully. There was a party I didn't want to miss and I thought it would be good for both of them to spend some quality time getting to know each other.

'Hey now, hang on a minute,' she said, blowing her cheeks out and shaking her head. 'I-I-I couldn't possibly. What if he needs to wee – or worse . . . ?' she asked, horrified. 'It was bad enough when you and your brother were babies . . .'

'He won't,' I said, stopping her before the subject of my infant nappies came up. I had to stifle a giggle as a picture of my mum poop-scooping after Gus popped into my head. 'I'll make sure he wees and poos before I bring him to you,' I reassured her. 'It'll only be for a couple of hours and he'll sleep for most of that time anyway.'

She hadn't said no yet, which was a good start, and I could tell she was thinking about it, which was really quite amazing!

'Oh, go on,' I said. 'You know you want to.'

She raised an eyebrow disapprovingly. 'Only for a couple of hours?' she asked. 'And you promise he'll sleep the whole time?'

'I promise. You won't even know you've got him!'

Unfortunately it didn't quite work out like that . . .

How was I to know there was going to be a thunderstorm next Saturday afternoon? As soon as the first crack of thunder broke, I left the party, jumped in the car and raced to my mum's flat. By the time I got there, she'd had Gus in thunderstorm mode for an hour.

I rang the bell. She opened the door and dragged me in. The first thing I noticed was the carpet by the front door had been pulled up. Poor Gus was trying to get out and escape the storm. He didn't realize he was better off inside.

The next thing I noticed was a puddle on the living-room floor. Oops. But none of that really mattered; it could all be cleaned up and fixed – I wanted to find my boy and make him see that everything was OK.

Gus was under the kitchen table, shaking like a blackcurrant jelly with ears. There was a pool of drool underneath him and he'd been sick too. When he saw me he ran to me, jumping up frantically as if to say, *Mumwherehaveyoubeen? WehavetogetoutofhereRIGHTNOW!!!!*

'Sshh, it's OK, boy,' I said, kneeling down to his level and stroking him. 'Quick, Mum, put a CD on.'

'A CD?' she said, confused. 'I don't think this is the time for dancing!'

'Quickly,' I urged. 'It'll drown out the sound of the thunder.'

The penny dropped and she scurried off. In the meantime, I ran for the windows and closed every single curtain in the flat to stop the lightning getting in. I sat on the floor with

Gus and he slowly began to calm down. That was until Take That came blaring through the speakers.

'Blimey, Mum, is that all you've got?'

'I could put Michael Bublé on if you think Gus would prefer it,' she replied.

'Never mind,' I said. 'This is fine, but can you turn it down a bit.'

When we'd all calmed down, Mum began to fill me in on what had happened. 'It began even before the clouds had properly gathered,' she said.

'That sounds about right,' I nodded. 'Dogs can detect a storm coming well before we can.'

'He started pacing up and down,' she continued, 'looking out the window and whimpering. You said he'd sleep the whole time – you *promised* me.'

'I didn't know there'd be a storm. What happened next?' I asked, wishing I hadn't.

'He started drooling everywhere,' she said,

pointing to various wet patches throughout the flat. The TV, the coffee table, the plants . . . in fact, the whole flat had been *Gus'd*. I thought back to that very first night I had him and knew exactly what she meant. 'And then he ran for the front door,' my mum added, 'and started pulling up the carpet! I didn't know what to do, so I brought him into the kitchen and made him some toast.'

'Toast?' I said, not quite understanding.

'Yes,' she said. 'I thought it might take his mind off the storm.'

'And did it?' I asked doubtfully.

'Yes, actually,' she said rather proudly. 'But then he threw it up!'

The storm took a while to pass, so we just sat there on the floor: Gus, my mum and me. Gus fell asleep with his head in my lap and my mum and I hummed along to Take That.

I was sure that this experience had put my mum off dogs for ever so no one was more surprised than me when she said, 'Poor Gus, he was so upset and I felt so helpless. You know, I even sat cuddling him for a while.'

I looked at her jumper and, sure enough, it had a few of Gus's black and grey hairs on it. My goodness, this really was something – my mum, cuddling a dog!

'But it was when I was cuddling him that he puked up his toast – all over my best shoes!'

Strangely enough, I think the two of them bonded that stormy afternoon, and in a funny sort of way they weren't all that different. Both loved a cup of tea, both owned a fur coat, and both enjoyed a bit of Take That!

Having my own dog was as brilliant as I knew it would be and I couldn't have wished for a better dog than Gus. For as long as I could remember, every single birthday and Christmas wish was taken up with *I wish that I had a dog*, and now finally I did.

I couldn't say what the absolute best thing was about having my own dog because there were so many best things, but here's an idea of some of them (in no particular order):

- having an extra best friend
- always having someone to talk to
- never feeling alone
- playing much more than I used to
- laughing much more than I used to
- going on fun walks
- learning new things about Gus every single day

I loved finding out all about Gus's own special quirks and characteristics. In some ways he was just like any normal dog; he liked to chew stuff (usually mine), he liked hanging out with other dogs, he'd drink out of the toilet given half the chance, and I found out the hard way (and so did my mum) that he was terrified of storms. In other ways, Gus was totally unique: his favourite food was bananas, he couldn't swim, he only had four teeth and one of his best friends was a ferret.

★

It was a cold, wet morning and the only people in the park were dog-owners walking their dogs . . . and their ferrets. Everyone was dressed in raincoats and wellies, and most carried umbrellas. Gus and Dusty weren't worried by the weather; quite the opposite, in fact. Val and I watched them race between the dripping trees, gallop through the sopping grass and whizz around the damp, deserted playground.

A little way past the playground I spied a rather large area of brown, wet, thick, gloopy mud. Uh-oh, this wasn't good. Val spotted it too.

'*Gus! Dusty!*' Val and I yelled at the same time.

Too late – they'd seen it and were racing off at top speed. As if it wasn't bad enough that Gus and Dusty were heading straight for the mud, suddenly Sally flew past us and went to join in the fun.

'Where did she come from?' Val asked me.

'No idea, but Mrs Bridgewater isn't going to like this,' I said.

'No, and she's bound to blame Gus and Dusty,' Val replied.

Gus was the first to dive in and was a little surprised at how deep it was. He stood from his paws right up to his chin in the brownish black muddy soup, dancing around and wagging his tail.

Dusty was in next; she bounded straight in without stopping and found herself swimming in it.

Sally stopped at the edge of the mud bath and hesitated.

Val and I looked around. Mrs Bridgewater was running at top speed towards the massive mud pie; Humphrey was jiggling up and down in her arms.

'*SALLY, DON'T YOU DARE!*' her owner screamed, racing towards her high-class hound. But Sally *did* dare – and Val, Mrs Bridgewater and I all looked on with our hands over our mouths as Sally reversed and produced one of the finest running jumps I'd ever seen.

The previously golden and spotlessly clean Sally was now covered from her chest to her toes in black syrup. As if that wasn't bad enough she nose-dived into the mud and disappeared completely! When she emerged, all we could see against the black muddy background were the whites of her eyes.

'*Gus!*' I yelled.

'*Dusty!*' Val squealed.

'*Sally!*' Mrs Bridgewater wailed.

Gus hadn't actually changed that much seeing as he was black to start with. Dusty, however, looked completely different to her former Weetabix self. She now looked more like a Coco Pop! And as for Sally, she no longer looked anything like the beautiful, elegant, clean pedigree she had been five minutes ago. Mrs Bridgewater held her head in her hands.

Then Humphrey must have decided it was unfair for the dogs to have all the fun because he suddenly leaped from Mrs Bridgewater's arms. We all watched aghast as he hurtled towards the mud bath.

'Oh no,' wailed Mrs Bridgewater, 'not you too!' But Humphrey was in, ducking and diving in and out of the mud, rolling around and covering himself in the thick gloop.

Val and I looked at each other, trying our best not to laugh, but our smiles were wiped off our faces when a large, angry-looking man came charging towards us, waving his arms around and yelling at Sally, '*Bruno! Bruno, you get out of there this minute!*'

Val and I were confused and even Mrs Bridgewater had stopped wailing. Then the man grabbed Sally, put a lead on her and began dragging her off. Mrs Bridgewater was so shocked she just stood there, frozen to the spot. Someone had to do something.

'Erm, excuse me,' I called over to the man, 'just where do you think you are taking Sally?'

'Sally?' he said, glancing down at the dog, looking even more confused than we were.

Just then a black Labrador came bouncing out of the bushes with a tree branch in his mouth. The branch was so long that Val and I had to jump in the air to avoid it! Sally pulled at the lead and managed to reach Bruno, grabbing one end of his stick. Side by side, they did look remarkably similar. Like Bruno, Sally was completely black from head to toe, they both had floppy ears and the same waggy tails. The man glanced from Sally to Bruno, Bruno to Sally, and then back to Sally once more.

Then the penny dropped. 'Ah, I get it,' I said to him. 'You thought Sally was your black Labrador.'

'Eh?' he replied, more confused than ever.

'It's an easy mistake to make,' I said, reassuring him he wasn't going mad. I pulled out a tissue and began wiping the mud off Sally's head. 'Sally is a golden retriever – she just looks like your dog because she's had a mud bath! See?' Sally's yellow head began to emerge from beneath my tissue.

'Well, would you believe it?' said the man, amazed. 'I could have sworn she was Bruno. I'd better get myself some glasses, and the quicker the better!'

A couple of months later I realized it wasn't just Bruno's owner who needed glasses. Something rather odd was happening at home.

Gus and I were off out for our usual morning stroll, but as we descended the twelve stairs from our flat to the ground floor, Gus decided to hurl himself down the last six.

'Hey!' I said, a little shocked. 'What are you doing? You'll break a leg, you silly old fool.' Assuming this was a one-off moment of madness I didn't think any more of it.

But the next day he did it again, and the day after that, and again the day after. It didn't seem to matter whose stairs they were or where we were; it was always the same story. I decided my dog must be going mad and wondered if the vet could explain this strange behaviour.

'Ah, Buzz,' Gus's white-whiskered doctor said as he stroked his white-whiskered patient, 'I haven't seen you for ages. What seems to be the trouble?'

'Well,' I said, 'I think Gus may be a little mad.'

'Oh?' said the vet, and turning to Gus asked, 'And what have you got to be a little sad about, Buzz? You've got a loving owner and a good home – it's more than some dogs have, you know.'

'No, not sad . . . *MAD!*' I shouted the last word. 'He's started jumping down long flights of stairs – it was eight steps the other day. I'm really worried he's going to break a leg.'

'Very odd,' said the vet. 'Well, pop him on the table and we'll have a good look at him.' The vet gave Gus a thorough examination starting with his heart. 'He's done very well to go on for so long with this heart murmur,' he said. 'How long have you had him now?'

'Almost two and a half years,' I replied.

'My, how time flies,' said the vet. 'It seems like only yesterday when he was still in the kennels and you brought him to me with that terrible case of kennel cough.'

I thought back to that snotty time and smiled at all the fun and adventures Gus and I had had since then.

'Yes, well,' said the vet, shifting from one foot to the other and coughing an embarrassed cough, 'these things are never exact, you know. All right, boy,' he continued, changing the subject, 'let's have a look at your pearly whites,' and he opened up Gus's mouth. 'His four teeth still look good and his breath is still acceptable.' Next he looked in Gus's ears. 'A bit of wax but nothing a ball of cotton wool won't clean out!'

The clean white fluffy cotton wool ball looked like a marshmallow when it went into

Gus's ear, but by the time it came out it looked more like a toasted marshmallow!

Then, using a special instrument with a light, the vet looked deep into Gus's eyes. 'Yes, just as I thought,' he said. 'Gus's eyes are failing him.'

My poor old boy. It suddenly struck me just how old Gus really was. I hadn't thought about it too much before because he never acted his age. He always seemed more like a puppy than a pensioner to me! But he was slowing down, all right, getting older, and the vet's diagnosis made perfect sense; Gus couldn't see the stairs properly so he couldn't judge how many were left. That was why he was throwing himself down the last few.

'What can we do to help him?' I asked, thinking hard. I'd never seen a dog wearing glasses before.

'I'm afraid there isn't anything we can do,' said the vet. 'You'll just have to help him slowly down stairs and make sure he takes just one at a time.'

And that's exactly what I did. Every time we came down any stairs I held tightly onto his collar and we counted down the stairs together. Slowly but surely, Gus learned that there were twelve stairs at our flat, and after a while I didn't have to hold his collar any more.

I often wondered if this meant Gus could count up to twelve. I'm still not sure – what do you think?

CHAPTER EIGHT

Gus Goes on Holiday

'Pack your things, Gus, we're going on holiday!' He carried on snoring. 'Oi, cloth ears,' I said to my sleepy hound, 'try not to get too excited!'

Gus had been my best friend for almost three years and to repay him for all his love, companionship, fun and friendship, I decided to take him to the seaside. The funny thing about Gus was that even though he couldn't swim and definitely didn't like going out of his depth, he loved the sea. He'd stand for ages just barking at the white frothy waves as they swept in and out, battering him all over the place.

But to Gus, the seaside meant more than just that big, wild, wet monster; it also meant Gran Gran. My granny (Gus's great-granny) was eighty-eight years old, but she didn't act a day over eight. She was fit, feisty and fun and had more energy than Gus and I put together!

When I first brought Gus home, Gran Gran was the only member of my family who threw her arms round him and gave him a big hug. It was love at first sight for both of them.

Gus continued snoring, so I tried a different approach. 'Wanna go see Gran Gran?' At the mention of his beloved great-granny, Gus opened his eyes. They were quite cloudy now and I knew he was beginning to rely more and more on his sense of smell than his eyesight. That was OK though, because dogs can smell hundreds of times better than we can, which is why they sniff absolutely everything: trees,

lampposts, the floor, other dogs' bottoms –
they're not fussy!

Gus got to his feet and stretched. That was
another thing I'd noticed; it was taking him
longer to get out of bed these days, and when
he did he was a little stiff. He had to have a
big long stretch and a good yawn to get going
properly.

'Oh, you poor old thing,' I said to him.
'Come here, boy, and I'll give you a massage.'
He staggered over and I massaged his neck, his
back and his legs. The vet said he had a bit of
arthritis and that the cold weather would make
it feel worse. No wonder he and Gran Gran got
on so well; they were both about the same age,
both had arthritis, both were a little deaf and
their eyesight wasn't what it used to be!

'Right,' I said to Gus when I'd given him
his massage, 'what do you want to take on
holiday?'

He shook one of his mighty shakes, ambled
into the kitchen for a slurp of water, and to

check his food bowl just in case some nice person had filled it up with yummy food while he was asleep. They hadn't, and he snorted the doggy version of a harrumph!

'Good idea, food bowl and water bowl,' I said. 'What else?' Gus had a scratch, turned around twice on the spot and lay down again. 'Well, *you're* not much help, are you!' It was autumn and getting colder, so I packed his warm grey woolly jumper. I also packed his waterproof coat, some poo bags, his bed, some dog food and treats, and his brush; Gran Gran loved to groom Gus.

The next morning we were up bright and early. I'd set the alarm way ahead of time because it took Gus so much longer to get going these days. It was a good thing he wasn't in charge of the snooze button or we'd never get out of the house!

After we'd had our breakfast we walked through the park on our way to the train station so that Gus could do his morning wee and poo.

As usual he made straight for the privacy of the bushes, and when he'd finished Sally and Humphrey were there to greet him.

'Morning, Gus,' said Mrs Bridgewater. 'What are you up to this weekend?'

Gus was too busy playing with his girlfriend so I answered on his behalf: 'We're off to the seaside to see Gus's great-granny.'

'I hope you've packed his coat,' said Mrs Bridgewater, 'as it's going to be cold this weekend and we don't want Gus's arthritis playing up, do we?' Mrs Bridgewater liked dogs more than she liked people and she'd become quite fond of Gus over the years. She didn't even mind him playing with Sally, her prized pedigree, any more. But she was still a little frosty with me. 'And no foolish ideas about leaping into freezing cold ponds – either of you!' she said to Gus and me.

Sally gave Gus a cheeky nip on the bum. He let out a yelp and began chasing her, which was exactly what she wanted. He caught up with her, but only because she let him; he was far too slow to catch her these days.

I looked at my watch. *Jeepers!* 'Come on, Gus,' I yelled, 'we've got to go!' I wasn't sure if he was ignoring me on purpose or whether he couldn't hear me, but we'd miss our train if we didn't get going. *'RIGHT NOW!'* I shouted at the top of my voice.

This did the trick but we were cutting it very fine. We ran to the station as fast as we could, which wasn't very fast in Gus's case. We charged through the big wide barriers for suitcases, prams and dogs, down one flight of stairs and up another. Platform 13 was certainly a long way from the station entrance and both Gus and I were getting puffed.

Halfway up the stairs I could see platform 13, but more alarmingly I could see that the train was already waiting there. Oh no, the guard was blowing his whistle!

'WAIT!' I yelled, and flung the closest door open so the train couldn't leave without us. I picked Gus up and threw him in, taking care not to drop him down the gap, and then I threw our bag and myself in. *Phew*, we'd made it — just!

I found a seat and settled down. Gus stretched out right across the aisle and promptly nodded off. Everyone who passed by stopped to ask if they could pat Gus, and the lady sitting opposite asked if he'd like a jammie dodger biscuit. Silly question, really! He wolfed it down, but the jammy bit got stuck on his tooth and I couldn't help laughing at the faces he pulled trying to dislodge it.

We arrived at Gran Gran's house and I rang the doorbell. Gus planted his nose in the keyhole, his tail wagging hard.

Gran Gran flung the door open, ignored me and threw her arms round Gus. 'Hello, boy,' she said, 'I've been waiting for you. Come in, there's a saucer of tea and a biscuit all ready for you.' She looked at me. 'He can have a biscuit, can't he?'

'Yes . . .' I replied. 'Hello, Gran Gran!'

'Oh yes, hello, darling!' she said, remembering I was there too. I didn't mind; I knew how much she loved Gus and that made me happy.

Gus always went straight into Gran Gran's kitchen to hoover up any food she might have unwittingly dropped, and he was usually rewarded with something. A few minutes later his hoovering habit got us all into a rather unusual predicament.

The three of us were sitting in the living room munching on snacks and happily nattering away. Gran Gran and I had crisps and cashew nuts, and Gus settled down to the chewy bone that Gran Gran had bought him from the pet shop. He kept a weather eye out for any crumbs Gran Gran might drop though, and as she and I chatted about what we'd been up to, her hearing aid fell out of her ear and landed at her feet.

Gus saw it too.

I knew exactly what was going to happen

next, but it happened so fast there was no way I could stop it.

'*Gus!*' I yelled. '*Nnnnoooo!*'

For all his aches and pains and arthritis, when he wanted to, Gus could move like lightning! I jumped out of my seat but Gus beat me to it. Thinking Gran Gran's hearing aid was a cashew nut (the two looked remarkably similar), Gus was on it, and before I could stop him, he'd swallowed it whole.

I pounced on him and prised his jaws apart. I put my fingers in his mouth and had a rummage around but it had disappeared down the hatch.

Gran Gran hadn't even realized her hearing aid had fallen out. 'What on earth are you doing?' she said, looking at me as though I'd gone stark raving mad.

'Your hearing aid just fell out and—'

'You'll have to speak up,' she said, 'this thing is playing up again,' and she put her fingers in her ear to adjust her hearing aid. 'Oh . . .'

'That's what I was trying to tell you,' I said,

almost having to shout. 'Your hearing aid fell out and Gus has eaten it!'

'Heavens above! He's eaten it?!'

I nodded. 'Swallowed it whole. Probably thought it was a cashew nut. I'll call your doctor and see if we can get a replacement.'

The doctor said there would be a three-week wait for the new hearing aid.

'I can't wait that long,' Gran Gran said.

I agreed, but there was only one alternative. 'We'll just have to wait for nature to take its course,' I said. 'It should only take a day or two,' I added helpfully.

Gran Gran and I looked at each other, and then at Gus who'd happily returned to chomping on his chew bone. This wasn't exactly a great start to our holiday.

The next morning I was up early and waited patiently for Gus and Gran Gran to surface. They got out of bed at roughly the same time, stretched, moaned, groaned . . . and farted.

After breakfast, the three of us donned our hats, scarves and coats and headed for the sea. It was blowing a gale outside, and being in charge of these two oldies was hard work; neither of them could hear properly and I had to hang on tight to both of them whenever we crossed the road.

I hadn't forgotten about Gran Gran's temporarily lost hearing aid and had a stash of poo bags at the ready. I always poop-scooped because it's the right thing to do, but I knew I'd have to squish Gus's poo through the bag to feel for any hard cashew-like objects. Let's hope it appeared sooner rather than later because I'd have to do this until the hearing aid finally emerged from deep within Gus.

We walked across a tree-lined field to reach the sea, and when Gus darted behind a tree I followed closely behind. He gave me a strange look – I must have put him off because he hurried along to the next tree. I watched intently, never letting him out of my sight, and when he'd done his business I ran over to pick up the poo.

I had a good feel through the bag. *Yuck!* It was warm and squashy but there was definitely no hearing aid. He looked up at me, probably wondering if I'd gone mad.

Gus only ever did one poo a day, so if the hearing aid was going to show itself we'd have to wait until tomorrow.

The three of us continued our journey. It was a wild and windy day and the sea was quite rough.

'Don't let him go in there,' Gran Gran said. 'It's too rough for him.'

'Don't worry,' I reassured her. 'He's a bit of a coward and never goes out too far. And he certainly won't go out of his depth.'

Gus happily trotted into the sea, just up to his ankles, and the white froth whooshed all around his legs, splashing him all over. He loved dancing in and out of the waves. His tail wagged and he barked his head off. I knew just by looking at him that this was Gus at his happiest.

'The wet will play havoc with his arthritis,' said Gran Gran. 'If I went in that sea I'd be stiff and achy for a week!'

'Lucky you haven't got your bikini then!' I shouted loud enough for her to hear.

Gus could have stayed in there all day, but I didn't want to tire Gran Gran out, so we headed for home and a nice hot bowl of soup.

On the way home, something most unusual happened. It must have been all that splashing around, but as we passed through the field Gus shot off behind the very furthest tree. This could only mean one thing; he was doing another poo.

I ran to keep up, but I couldn't see him until he bounded out, wagging his tail. I knew this happy little display meant he'd done another poo, but where on earth was it? It was autumn so hundreds of leaves carpeted the grass; spotting one poo in amongst them would be very difficult. I searched and searched while Gran Gran threw a stick for Gus.

I'd almost given up when . . . *squelch!* I felt something soft under my left foot. Normally I'd be horrified if I trod in doggy-doo, but at that moment I was delighted. I carefully extracted my shoe from the poo in case the hearing aid was under it and bent down to have a look. I squeezed my nose shut and knelt down for a closer inspection.

'Gran Gran,' I shouted, 'it's here. I've got it!'

I scooped it up in a bag and the three of us hurried home. Gus flopped down in front of the fire to dry off and Gran Gran made the soup for lunch. I, on the other hand, had the unenviable task of cleaning up the hearing aid. Using cotton buds, an old toothbrush, bleach, disinfectant, washing-up liquid and a little water, I got to work.

For the next hour I worked slowly and painstakingly, only stopping for a quick bowl of soup. Gran Gran had her soup and fed Gus a banana before settling down to groom him. By the time I'd finished, Gus's coat shone like a sea lion's and the hearing aid looked as good as new too; in fact, it looked better than new. But would it actually work?

I handed Gran Gran the hearing aid and she popped it back in her ear as though nothing had happened. I waited to see if any damage had been done. This was probably the first time a hearing aid had ever travelled the entire length of a dog and I wasn't sure it would stand up to the test!

'Testing testing,' I said in a whisper. 'Earth to Gran Gran, come in, Gran Gran,'

'This is Gran Gran,' she replied. 'Go ahead, Earth.'

We both laughed like a couple of hyenas, amazed and delighted it still worked.

'Brilliant; no harm done,' I said, relieved.

'What? You want a bun?' she replied. Oh no; the hearing aid hadn't survived after all. 'Only teasing,' Gran Gran said. 'It's as good as new!'

*

The rest of our holiday was less eventful, thank goodness, but no less enjoyable and I hoped Gus had a good time. I'm sure he did; after all, he was hanging out with his two favourite people who were both spoiling him rotten. He was eating all his favourite foods, going on interesting walks, being groomed by his great-granny and splashing about in his beloved sea.

Do you think Gus had a good holiday?

CHAPTER NINE

Puppy Pandemonium

I often wonder what would have happened to Gus if I hadn't rescued him from the kennels all those years ago. Perhaps some nice old man would have taken him home; two granddads together in their knitted jumpers, enjoying a cup of cocoa before bed.

Maybe Jimmy Stickles would have come out of prison, picked him up from the dogs' home and Gus would be back to his old car-stealing ways!

Maybe he'd *still* be stuck in that draughty old kennel. But he wasn't; Gus was in his rightful place here with me, all warm and snug, asleep in his bed.

'Gus . . . wake up, Gus, I've got something to tell you,' I said to my sleeping hound. 'We're looking after a puppy for two days. Her name's Pinky and she's arriving later today.'

SNOOORRRRE! SNOOORRRRE!

'Fine,' I said, 'but don't say I didn't warn you.'

An hour later the doorbell rang. I went downstairs to open the door, and before I knew it a small brown-and-white blur shot past me and bounded up the stairs. From what I could make out the puppy was about the size of a cat, but unlike a cat she had long dangly brown ears.

'Manners, Pinky!' her embarrassed owner shouted after the young bouncy springer spaniel.

'How's the training going?' I asked, but

before Pinky's owner had a chance to reply, the answer unfolded before my own two eyes. Pinky was now on the top step, with a look of intense concentration on her face. It took me a few seconds to realize she was having a wee.

'Oh, you know . . .' her owner replied a little sheepishly. A bag containing Pinky's lead and collar, her food and water bowls, her blanket and teddy bear, was thrust into my hand. 'Thanks for having her – see you in two days.'

And just like that, she was gone. Oh, why did I ever agree to this?

AAWWOOOOLLLPPHH! That sounded like Gus. I slammed the front door and raced upstairs to find Pinky bouncing all over him. She looked delighted to have a furry playmate. Gus, on the other hand, seemed less enthusiastic.

'That's what I was trying to tell you, Gus,' I explained as I peeled Pinky off his head. 'Pinky is staying with us for two days. That's forty-eight hours – no, hang on . . .' I looked at my ticking watch. 'Actually, it's only another forty-seven hours and fifty-six minutes.'

Gus sighed a long weary sigh.

Just then, Pinky ran around in three tight circles, squatted and pooed right where she stood, on my living-room carpet. When she'd finished, she trotted into the kitchen and hoovered up the end of Gus's breakfast, which he always saved for his mid-morning snack.

Gus and I looked at each other; this was going to be a long two days . . .

Puppies have boundless energy, and as I watched Pinky race around the flat, jumping on chairs, bed, sofa, table, I realized we had to get out of there.

Gus knew the routine, and as I put my coat on he sat patiently underneath his collar and lead, which hung by the front door. I dressed him without any fuss and we turned our attention to Pinky, who was busy chewing the arm of my sofa.

'Pinky, *no!*' I said, diving to save my furniture. With one hand I restrained the squirming puppy, and with the other I delved into her bag and pulled out her collar and lead. This sent her into a frenzy of excitement and she threw herself at me, trying to push her head into her collar to speed things up, but instead she became tangled up in the bag.

'No, Pinky,' I said, 'wait; hang on a sec. *You're not helping!* Just sit still!'

Gus looked on, unimpressed, probably thinking it was my own fault for agreeing to have a puppy in the house. He had a point.

'You're right,' I said to him. 'This is exactly the reason we don't do puppies, and that's why I brought *you* home three and a half years ago instead of a young loony like this!'

I wrestled Pinky into her collar and lead and the three of us finally made it outside. As we walked along the street I noticed Pinky looking up at Gus, following his every move. This was a good start. Her owner had told me she pulled like crazy on the lead, but because Gus always walked right by my side and never pulled, Pinky was copying him.

Do you think she saw him as her new big brother?

Thankfully there were fences all around the park, so it was safe to let Pinky off the lead for a run around. We had to get rid of all that puppy energy somehow or my flat, not to mention my poor Gus, would never survive the next two days.

I let the dogs off their leads at the same time and, as usual, Gus made for the bushes. He didn't quite bound these days; it was more of an amble to find the perfect spot for his daily poo. Pinky stuck to him like glue.

'Oh, Pinky,' I said, 'give him a bit of space; some things are private!' Not that *she* thought so, having just publicly poo'd in our living room!

I wandered off towards the coffee hut, and as I was ordering a hot chocolate my phone rang; it was my mum.

'Hello, darling,' she said. 'Do you and Gus want to come and have lunch with me today?' A part of me still couldn't believe my mum was happy to have a dog in her house.

'That would be lovely,' I replied, 'but I'm looking after a puppy – can she come too?'

The phone went dead. I'll take that as a *no*, then. Mum was obviously only happy to have one dog in her home; a very particular and special dog who goes by the name of General Gus. She had good taste, my mum.

I turned round to see how the dogs were getting on. Oh no! They'd wandered off together in the opposite direction and were now quite some distance away.

'Gu–us!' I called. He and Pinky were chatting to an enormous Great Dane. Pinky looked like a mouse in his huge shadow. 'GU–US!' I yelled, this time a little louder.

His hearing was worse than ever and his eyesight wasn't too good either, but to my surprise and delight he lifted his head up and looked around.

'Over here,' I shouted, waving. But he shot off in the other direction towards a complete stranger, with Pinky following behind her new best friend. As Gus reached the stranger he wagged his tail hard, thinking it was me. When he got no response from the lady he sniffed her to make sure it was me. That was when the penny dropped. Thank goodness his sense of smell was as sharp as ever. I called him again; he looked around and changed course – but once again in the wrong direction.

Then something extraordinary happened. Pinky, who knew exactly where I was, began to herd Gus towards me, a bit like a sheepdog herding sheep!

'Good girl!' I said, patting the pup when they reached me. 'You could be Gus's new guide dog!' I turned to my old soldier. 'And where were you running off to?' I asked him.

They both deserved a treat; Pinky for returning Gus to me, and Gus for being deaf but brilliant. I knelt down to their level. 'Sit,' I said, rummaging in my bag to find them both a treat.

Gus sat perfectly but Pinky jumped up, slamming the top of her head into my jaw, causing me to bite my tongue.

'*Ooowwww!*' I wailed.

Pinky thought this was some sort of doggy howl and joined in too! '*Ooowwww*,' she howled.

'Sit,' I repeated. Gus's bum was already on the ground, but he did a little shuffle to make sure I'd noticed. I gave him a treat but wanted to wait until Pinky's bum was on the grass before I'd give her one too.

She was bouncing around like a tennis ball – until she accidentally bounced on Gus's tail. He'd had enough of this unruly toddler and let out a sound somewhere between a squeal and a growl. It was enough to stop Pinky in her tracks. She'd never been told off by another dog before and she sat as still as a furry statue, a little afraid of her older, larger playmate.

This was working out very well; Pinky was showing Gus how to find me in the park and, in return, Gus was showing Pinky how to behave! I gave her the treat; it didn't touch the sides.

We walked home with Pinky once again shadowing Gus and walking very well to heel. As I opened the downstairs front door Pinky raced to the top of the stairs and waited for Gus and me. We caught up with her and I unlocked our front door. Pinky shot through the door as though something very exciting lay on the other side.

'That's annoying,' I said to myself – I'd dropped Gus's coat at the bottom of the stairs. 'Stay here, boy,' I said to him. 'I'll go back down and get it. No use both of us getting puffed.' I trudged down the stairs, picked up the coat and that was when it happened . . .

I heard the upstairs front door slam! Oh no. The keys were inside, but even worse than that – *so was the puppy!!!!* I raced up the stairs to Gus, who was sniffing the bottom of the door and looking back at me as if to say, *uh-oh!*

Uh-oh was about right. I put my ear to the door. 'Pinky?' I called. She began barking wildly. 'Sshh,' I said, trying not to disturb the neighbours. How could this be happening? She must have accidentally knocked the door shut. I'd thrown the keys on the sofa as soon as I'd unlocked the door. Oh, why hadn't I just kept them in my hand?

Right; think. Don't panic, think. The barking stopped and it had gone eerily quiet inside my flat. This was even more worrying than the barking. My mind raced, imagining all the things she could be getting up to. I put my ear to the door.

'Pinky?'

RRRIIIIIIIIPPPPPPPPP!

What was that? It sounded like material

ripping. My sofa? My carpet? My clothes? My duvet?

Silence once again.

Gus looked up at me; he knew this wasn't good.

SSMMMAAASSSSSSHHHH!!!

This was getting serious. Think, think, think. Spare keys? Yes. Who's got them . . . ? Think, think, th—

SSMMAAASSSHHHH!!!

Gus let out a long whine.

'I know, Gus, *I know*; she's destroying our home!' I needed to get her away from . . . from . . . well, everything really. 'Pinky,' I wailed, trying to get her to come to the door. At least if she was just on the other side of the door, she couldn't be wrecking the flat. *Wrong!*

RRIIIPPP!

She was back on the other side of the door, but now the carpet beneath the door was taking a battering. Gus began pawing at the door.

'You're right, boy; we have to get in there,' I agreed.

Think! Quick! Who did I give the spare keys to? My brother who lives just round the corner? That would have been the smart thing; I could have run round to his house and been back in five minutes. But no, I didn't do the smart thing. I'd given them to my mum who lived twenty minutes away in the car. OK, twenty minutes isn't so bad; it could be worse.

'Come on, Gus, *hurry*!' I said as I raced back down the stairs, flinging open the front door. Gus followed, counting down the twelve steps to the bottom. I heard him moan. 'I know, I know, but just think; at this time in two days it'll all be over – Pinky will have gone home.' This didn't seem to help and he trudged over to the car.

My hand searched my pocket, and then it dawned on me. *The car keys were locked in my flat too!!!!!!* Just then the car door unlocked all on its own. *Eh?* I looked at Gus. He looked at me. Oh no; Pinky must be chewing the car key! The car locked again. I looked up to my living-room window, half expecting to see Pinky waving back.

I sat on the kerb with my head in my hands as I heard another crash coming from my flat. Gus nudged my elbow up and snuggled his head under my arm. That was just what I needed; a dog-hug from my favourite dog.

'We could have been at your granny's now,' I moaned to Gus, 'having a civilised lunch.' At the mention of his granny's name, Gus began wagging his tail and licking my face. 'Wait! That's it!' I said. 'We're saved!' I fumbled in my pocket to get my phone. At least I still had that.

'Mum; emergency!' I said.

'What is it?' she asked.

'Gus and I are locked out of the flat.'

'That's not an emergency,' she sighed.

'It is when there's a puppy loose in there!'

'Oh my goodness,' she said, immediately

realizing the horror of the situation. 'Who's got your spare keys?'

'You have,' I replied.

'I'm on my way.' *Brilliant!* Thank goodness for mums.

She must have driven like Lewis Hamilton because she arrived at my doorstep ten minutes later. My mum didn't know much about dogs – but she knew that a puppy locked alone in a flat wasn't good.

She handed me the spare set of keys and the two of us ran up the stairs, with Gus following behind. I put my ear to the door.

Silence.

I placed the spare key in the lock and pushed the door open. It was just like rewinding my life three and a half years to the first night I had Gus; only worse – much, much worse. At least there was no snot; but what Pinky lacked in kennel cough, she made up for in every other department.

She had:

- pulled the tablecloth off the table . . .

which led to:

- the vase toppling off . . .

which led to:

- water, daffodils and tulips all over the carpet.

This in turn led to:

- wet paw prints everywhere.

She had also:

- ripped up the cushions on the sofa but thankfully left the sofa intact, which was lucky, because faced with this scene my mum felt faint and needed somewhere to sit.

Pinky had also:

- dug up the plants

which led to:

- soil on the carpet

which led to:

- muddy paw prints *everywhere*!

And that was just the living room.

I followed the paw prints, which led me to the bedroom where I found the culprit. Pinky was lying on my bed, surrounded by daffodils and tulips. The white duvet was now spotted with black paw prints and it looked like a giant Dalmatian was lying across my bed. She had chewed my pillows and had so many feathers stuck to her damp little body that she resembled a duck.

My mum walked into the bedroom and promptly walked out again. In fact, she walked out of the flat, got into her car and drove off saying she could feel one of her headaches coming on. I didn't blame her. If I could have walked out of there I would have too.

I put Pinky in the bathroom – there was nothing she could destroy in there – and set about the clean-up operation. Thinking it was probably best to keep out of the way, Gus took himself off to his bed in the only un-Pinky'd corner of the living room. I looked at my watch.

'Right, boy,' I said to Gus. 'For the next forty-four hours and twenty-eight minutes we'll have to take turns on Puppy Watch. I'll take the lion's share, but while I'm in the shower you're in charge, OK?'

Gus wagged his agreement.

Between Gus and I standing guard, our remaining time with Pinky actually went quite well (if you don't count the twenty-pound note she chewed into thirty pieces). In the park she continued to act as Gus's guide dog, and at home he was her guard dog.

Two days later Gus and I handed Pinky back to her owner. We closed our front door on the outside world (and naughty puppies) and settled back into our own comfortable, peaceful, un-chewed life together. Forty-eight hours with a four-legged toddler was more than enough for the both of us!

As Gus slept contentedly beside me without fear of being bounced on, I looked into his old grey face and wondered how much time he and I had left together. He was my faithful furry friend, but dogs grow older seven times faster than people and it's true what they say – all good things must come to an end.

About three months after Pinky came to stay, Gus passed away peacefully in his sleep. He was thirteen and a half, which is nearly ninety-four in human years!

I don't know what he spent his first ten years doing (apart from stealing cars!), but I do know that for the last three and a half years of his life Gus was very happy — and so was I.

AFTERWORD

Dogs can live for up to sixteen years. I rescued Gus when he was quite old, so I didn't have him that long, but what we lacked in time together we made up for in fun, adventures, companionship and love.

Most people visiting rescue centres want puppies and young dogs, but older dogs shouldn't be forgotten or passed by; they deserve a second chance to have a happy life too. Their eyesight might not be what it once was and their hearing could be a little better, but their need to love and be loved is as strong as it always was. Oldies have charm, manners and bundles of character. They are well-behaved, cute and always have a story to tell.

Sound like anyone you know?

Gus was my first dog and I'll never forget him. How could I? Without Gus, I never would have had to wipe snot off everything I owned, worn earplugs at night to drown out his snoring and I definitely wouldn't have jumped into a freezing cold lake! Without Gus, my mum would never have realized just how wonderful dogs really are and those school children might have grown up always being afraid.

My next dog will be a rescue dog. I don't know if it'll be a boy or a girl, what breed, size or colour it will be. But I do know without any doubt that my next dog will be an oldie.

Why? Because Gus showed me that you *can* teach an old dog new tricks!